More praise for
Roses, Roses and Bill James

"The restless, spiky style of James's brilliant dialogue was never more appropriate; the rose blooms without a hint of melodrama."   —*Oxford Times*

"Bill James is a crime writer who attracts discriminating fans who are not content with the ultimately unsatisfying blockbuster. . . . Utterly absorbing."   —Frances Fyfield

"Bill James's Harpur and Iles books are deliciously unsavoury: a brilliant combination of almost Jacobean savagery and sexual betrayal with a tart comedy of contemporary manners."   —John Harvey
          "The Crime Writer's Crime Writer," *Guardian*

"There is a terrifying credibility about this series that makes so many of its rivals seem trivial by comparison."
                          —*Manchester Evening News*

"Masterly. . . . There is nothing else quite like this series of police procedurals. James is concerned with the dilemmas and difficulties of policing Britain's inner cities, and he addresses these in hard-edged narratives that leave readers gasping and flinching. . . . It's all delivered in a ferociously poetic voice that is uniquely Bill James."
          —*The* [London] *Times*, "100 Masters of Crime"

"[A] remarkable series. . . . To say this series is unique is to use the adjective properly."   —*D̶e̶a̶d̶l̶y̶*

By Bill James in Foul Play Press

Roses, Roses

Bill James

A Foul Play Press Book

W. W. Norton & Company
New York   London

For information about permission to reproduce selections of this book,
write to Permissions, W. W. Norton & Company, Inc., New Yotk, NY 10110

First published 1993 by Macmillan London Limited
Copyright © Bill James 1993

First published as a Foul Play Press paperback 1999
First published 1998 by Foul Play Press, a division of
W. W. Norton & Company, New York

Printed in the United States of America

A CIP catalogue record for this book is available from
the British Library

Library of Congress Cataloging-in-Publication Data
James, Bill. 1929–
    Roses, roses / Bill James. — 1st American ed.
    p.   cm
    ISBN 0-393-04637-0
    I. Title.
PR6070.U23R67   1998
823'.914—dc21   98-17693
                                                        CIP

ISBN 0-393-31925-3 pbk.
W. W. Norton & Company, Inc.
500 Fifth Avenue, New York, NY 10110
www.wwnorton.com

W. W. Norton & Company Ltd.
10 Coptic Street, London WC1A 1PU

1 2 3 4 5 6 7 8 9 0

Chapter 1

When she was killed by three chest knife blows in a station car park, Megan Harpur had been on her way home to tell her husband she was leaving him for another man. Now and then, and lately more often, she went up to London on what she called shopping and theatre trips, and which did fit in shopping and theatre, and returned by the last train, arriving at 1.22 a.m. There would be a handful of other passengers with their Selfridges or Harrods carrier bags who left the train, too, but at that hour Megan was generally the only one travelling alone, and always the only woman travelling alone. She had four carrier bags herself. One of them contained presents for her daughters, Hazel and Jill, and, as it happened, one for Colin, her husband. None of her purchases appeared to have been taken, though some had been stacked tidily near her on the ground: these included the presents and a pair of bold patterned cotton trousers for herself, plus a sale tablecloth in cheerfully embroidered Irish linen. The tablecloth took most of the staining. This washed out fine, and as soon as it was released by Forensic, the girls suggested sending it with Megan's clothes to Oxfam. They were good kids, who thought they should contain their grief, keep it under, partly for Harpur's sake, partly to strengthen each other; but now and then some reminder of Megan would touch them in a way they could not control or hide. The tablecloth was like that, and together they decided it had better go.

Harpur said they should keep it, use it. Of course he understood and more or less shared their pain, but also wished them to learn early that you could not let death run you ragged, not anyone's death.

'I don't want people crowing,' he said.

'Who'd know?' Jill asked.

'These people, they know.'

'That's stupid. Melodramatic,' Hazel remarked.

'Which people?' Jill asked.

'I'll find them.'

'Maybe,' Hazel said. 'London people or local?'

'I'll find them.'

'You're that interested?' Hazel asked. 'Just as a cop?'

'They're crowing anyway,' Jill said.

'If you don't like it, I'll always sit at that end of the table,' he replied. Harpur had on the tie Megan was bringing back for him, which had also been released. Silk, it was a terrible, wan, middle-management thing, but had to be honoured. This, too, was stained, with engine oil from the car park surface, not blood. The black blemish was at a spot that could not be hidden, and he felt glad he had no reputation as a fashion plate to nurse.

Chapter 2

'A fucking watershed, Harpur, no less.' The Assistant Chief stood behind his desk, glibly turned out in a brilliant double-breasted grey suit, and what would probably be one of his rugby club ties decorated with small, deeply unflashy silver shields. 'I have to tell you I did a thorough morgue glance at the body, Col.'

'Sir, if you thought you might be taking the case—'

'I had a right, a duty to look. Yes,' Iles replied, nodding. 'I'd still like to clear it with you, after the event and while we're alone. Naturally, you're going to ask whether, if this had been the Chief's old double wardrobe of a wife, I would have wanted to pull back the slab sheet and commit an ogle. Touché, of course, Harpur.' Iles grew, for him, preposterously delicate. 'I don't know how many bodies I've had to look at in my day, Col, but with Megan it seemed an intrusion. This was a life I respected, whatever you might say about her. For instance, if things were reversed, it would infinitely nauseate me to think you, Harpur, were squinting at Sarah in that state, even though you must repeatedly have gazed on her when—'

'Megan did have three wounds, sir, as first thought?' Harpur replied.

'Yes, that's right, Harpur, do your detective chief super bit and reduce things to post-mortem terms, won't you?'

'All I've got.'

The ACC carried out some significant pacing between desk and window. 'Obviously, as husband you were right not to handle the case yourself, Col – unthinkable – but, yes, I have wondered whether Francis Garland can cope, pretty as his talent may be, and almost as pretty as he thinks. Didn't I say

3

on the actual night in the car park that one might look at it personally? One has these occasional juvenile longings for the sharp end again.'

'Sir, I—'

'It's kind of you to suggest one will be overworked, but I insist. Naturally, you'll ask what I mean by "watershed". Well, the States is another item, but what we do not have and will not have in this country is cops' as it were loved ones used by villains as means of retaliation or foul pressure. I'll put the stopper on that at once. Loss of a dear wife – who can say what that might do to a man? I've tried to imagine how it would be if this had happened to Sarah. She's sauntered out a bit from the strictly wedded now and then, as you know, and so does Garland, of course, yet she could not but be central to me at all times.

'I think Megan was about to leave me, sir.'

The Assistant Chief smoothed his fine grey hair and for a moment fell into classic interrogator's style, beautifully fabricating a multi-stage question that reached its own answer. 'Leave? That provoke you, enrage you, make you desperate, make you, yes, murderous, Harpur?' He seemed to realize what he was doing and switched back to colleague talk. 'Brain-dead slob, should you be telling me this if I'm doing the inquiry? Women, they terrorize us, Col.'

'But things seem to have sorted themselves out for you and Sarah.'

'They get their eternal, impossible urgings. The poor dears are helpless, ruthless. You'd think the way they're made they'd be able to sit on their feelings, but, no, simply this frantic build of secret heat, like a blaze in a rick. And they've come to want to live the way we do, some of them.'

'Perhaps that's natural.'

'Oh, we don't believe that, do we, Harpur?'

Chapter 3

On the way back in the train, Megan had rehearsed what she would say to Colin.

You've seen it coming. You won't care. It's just a matter of who made the break first.

She would try to wait until the kids were out of the house, because this would be a full-voice session. Neither of them believed in the 'we were intelligent people' stuff, 'no tears no fuss'. When you were tearing and being torn, you yelled. There had been earlier instalments of this, though never going all the way. If you ripped something to bits, let's hear it come apart.

You can handle an open marriage. So can I if I have to, and now I've decided I don't have to.

She kept it terse, because when you were shouting, snarling, you had to sound sure. He spent his grubby professional life combing words for frailties.

You betrayed me first.

And she felt sixty per cent certain this was right. He would not argue, would find timetabling ludicrous. He had a point, when it was a matter of destroying a family. She would say it, all the same. She had to feel justified, or not completely unjustified. There was a lot of her life left and she could not carry a barrel of blame for the next thirty-five years, not even forty per cent of a barrel of blame.

Seated there in the almost empty train, formulating, she could gaze along the length of her brightly lit carriage, then the next and even part of the next. That view had helped make Megan think of her life stretching far ahead, bright, too: a bit like the unending corridors in her surreal video, *L'Année*

Dernière à Marienbad, which she loved and which Colin naturally denounced as pretentious bullshit. A man sat in the next but one carriage, almost at the limit of her vision, apparently gazing towards her, as she gazed towards him. It was too far to make out much. He had on dark clothes, sat straight, could be young, might have a small, dark moustache. There was communication, there was no communication: capsuled people. Perhaps he wondered who she was, travelling alone, as she wondered who he was, travelling alone, and possibly with a fur collar to his overcoat. Probably, he was not looking at her at all. He might even be asleep, despite that upright posture. The distance was too great to see his eyes: one of those situations where you hoped a man, maybe a youngish man, felt interested in you, appreciated your appearance even from afar, and spotted depths, and also hoped he didn't. It might have troubled Megan had he stood up and made his way towards her. Once or twice Colin had asked her about the wisdom of coming in late by train so often, so regularly. It was his training to see the world as menace and believe there were people charting your movements. He never pushed it – couldn't, because this would be using safety points to keep her tied. He would despise that. The man stayed where he was, of course.

She knew she ought to work out what she would say to Colin about the children, but could not find the phrasing. There were no right words for that. If he had been as tender to her as he was to them she might not be preparing an exit speech now, rattling and swaying through these sleeping nowhere spots, wondering if her beauty carried the length of a couple of railway carriages and at least a decade.

Yes, I'm going to Tambo. Who else? He's very insistent. Don't bloody laugh. Someone wants me. Then a pause. *Yes, it is a bit of a giggle, I suppose, Col.* The nickname took away some of the gravity, of course. But it had stuck, after he played Tamburlaine the Great in an amateur society show when he still worked here, before his move to the Met. The name, hatched in the police canteen, probably, was derisive, naturally, and meant to make him sound part like that loud dictator and part like the Rambo wild man. Thank God, he was not either.

6

Chapter 4

Harpur himself had found Megan's body, tucked in against her Astra and humped over some of the purchases, the rest nearby, out of the bags but tidy. Perhaps not just a body: he thought she might still be alive and lifted her with all the tenderness he could on to the back seat of his ageing Granada and talked to her with all the tenderness he could for all the seven-minute journey to Casualty at the Paston, where eventually a black girl doctor came to Waiting and announced dead on arrival with a kindly whisper in his ear, her breath rich Wrigley. Casualty was in a smart, new, cheery wing of the Paston, with nursery rhyme pictures on the walls to beguile hurt children. He was sitting alongside a couple of mangled, white tap-room scrappers in their fifties and the three of them had a thick sprinkle of blood across their shoes, the other two's their own. This pair had not been gracious about Megan's going ahead of them into Treatment, but Harpur felt they had enough injuries for their age and listened to the boozed protests and threats without response.

He had telephoned while Megan was examined and reported his find. For job anonymity he always used old cars without a radio, otherwise on their way to the hospital he might have been able to ask Control to call ahead and get things a bit more ready. What did it mean 'on arrival'? It meant when they had a proper look at her in there, and how long did that take? Was the nice young doctor on the spot immediately or at the all-night canteen for more gum? The Granada had rattled its worn-out frame and the engine came over loud at between a whine and a rasp, but above it all he thought he heard some sort of sound from Megan: a little, dim, miserably brief struggle for oxygen or even an attempt to speak. 'I hear you, love,' he said. He was used to hearing her. His soaked hands slipped about on the wheel. He realized that calling her 'love' meant less than if he had used her name. He might have addressed any woman dying in the back of his car as love. There was a distance between Megan and him that not even a knife could cut short. He drove as hard as the Granada would take. He would do that for anyone.

Normally, Harpur would have slept through and not gone to find why she was late. But he did not get home himself until nearly 2.45 a.m. and was troubled to see her car still missing from the drive. He had been looking at a burgled fashion shop in the town centre and when he returned to the house made a couple of telephone calls about the likelies to be picked up, then mixed himself a weighty gin and cider, the weight mainly gin. By the time he went to bed it was 3.30 and, despite the drink, he lay awake listening for Megan. This time, and a couple of times before, it had struck him when she left on a London trip that she might have decided to go for good. It would not be like her to slink away with no statement – she loved statements – but he feared it was possible. Yes, feared it: the unmistakeable finality. He hated definition, lived by ambiguity.

At just after four o'clock Hazel came into the bedroom and said she had woken up and looked out and Megan's car was not there. Why had she looked? Perhaps the child also sensed Megan might quit one of these days or nights. Perhaps Megan had said so. He did not ask. Harpur pretended he had been at peace and sleeping, grunted a bit in supposed confusion and said he would drive to the station in case she had car trouble. If she had car trouble and had come in nearly three hours ago she would have telephoned or called a taxi, but he needed to make some effort and Hazel seemed to need him to make some effort, too, although she also would see the absurdity. It was what families were about.

'You stink of booze. Are you over the limit, Dad?'

'Probably.'

'Ah, well, who's going to breathalyse C. Harpur?'

'Some would.'

'Yes, some of your friends are enemies.'

'That's what's known as a job description.'

The car park was unlit, a long tree-bordered rectangle, narrowing at one end towards a path and footbridge across the line. A few cars stood in the spaces, owners away for more than one night. He saw her Astra at once, ten metres from a grey Volvo, and could make out something wide and white fluttering in the wind, occasionally curling around to the front of the Astra and dragging across the bumper and number plate, like a loose sail. He accelerated, arcing out then straightening to point his headlights directly into the gap between the two cars. He saw Megan lying near some of her shopping, including the tablecloth, which had part unfolded so one end was lifted by the gusts and blown against the vehicle. Other, more solid, items – books, a couple of CDs, porcelain in a box, a small framed print or picture – had been placed on the ground near her legs. As he left the car and approached her, Harpur heard a sudden, insistent rushing, rustling sound from among the trees and turned urgently to look that way and guard himself. He saw what must be one of her carrier bags, green and substantial, caught up by its handle-string high in a bush, crackling and ballooning in the breeze. His panic sickened him: never mind your flattened wife, think of your skin.

Megan was on her side and he crouched down close, noticing the concentration of blood high on her yellow sweater. Her eyes were shut. She lay on a paperback encyclopedia she had bought, so her body was slightly raised at the hips, though her right cheek rested flat on the ground. There were small black stones in her hair. At that stage he did not speak. At that stage he was capable and followed routine and training. He behaved like a policeman and like a *compos mentis* husband. Taking her left wrist he felt for a pulse and thought yes, far off, very slow and slowing more, even in the few moments he held her. He tried for a neck pulse, too, but could find nothing there. He hurried back to the Granada, opened the rear door and swept all the junk off the back seat except for an old sweater. Then he picked up Megan and carried her to it, laying her down still on her side, her head supported by

9

the folded sweater. One thing about the Granada – most women could stretch out on the back full-length. He had already known that. All the same, he closed the door gingerly so as not to catch her, then drove.

Later, after the doctor's private announcement, there was some paper work, which she handled. 'Name of deceased.'

'Megan Irene Harpur.'

'Address of deceased.'

'126 Arthur Street.'

'Age of deceased.'

'Thirty-six.'

'Identified by.'

'Colin Harpur.'

'Relationship to deceased.'

'Husband.'

'Occupation.'

'Police officer.'

'Yes? We are asked though not required to supply information about the nature of the occurrence.'

'You tell me.'

'At least three deep wounds in the chest, either of which could have killed, Mr Harpur. In my judgement. Is it all right if I call you mister? But when they ask the nature of the occurrence they mean how the wounds, well, occurred, Mr Harpur.'

'She was knifed in a car park.'

'Were you present, Mr Harpur?'

'Look, *I'm* the detective. These were skilled blows?'

'Mr Harpur, your wife is dead. You must see her, please. This is to confirm the identification.' She led him to a small room and switched on the light. There were two stretcher trolleys. On one a body was covered totally by a sheet. On the other, Megan lay with the sheet folded back at the neck. She looked as she almost always looked, beautiful and remote, her mouth aggressive, as though about to snarl at him again about his contemptible use of informants, or some other unclean bit of police method. The doctor eased her chewing rate out of respect.

'Yes,' he said.

The girl covered Megan's face and switched out the light. 'I'll ask you to sign the identification, Mr Harpur.' They went to an office containing four desks heaped with papers and files and she cleared a space on hers and gave him a pen. In the corridor outside, one of the pub fighters walked back towards Waiting, his head bandaged and big plasters on two face cuts. Seeing Harpur through the open door, he stopped, half entered, squaring up his body to look burlier, the jolly wreck, transmitting down-grade fumes.

'We'll be waiting for you outside, queue-jumping, posh ponce,' he said.

Harpur reached across suddenly and ripped one of the plasters from his face. The man staggered back and groaned, his wound spouting gorgeously. Harpur made as if to pull the other plaster off, but the man covered his face with both hands. 'No, I shouldn't wait, if I were you,' Harpur replied. 'You've lost blood and need rest. My friend here will fix you up with a new dressing.'

'You must be quite high ranking,' the doctor replied.

Harpur had a wash and sponged his clothes in the hospital lavatory, then drove back out to the car park. The area was busy with police now and some early commuters. Two batteries of emergency lights had been set up near where he found Megan. A miserable December dawn was breaking. The goods she had bought lay as before, except that the tablecloth was properly folded and held in place by a large police flashlight. From where he stood, Harpur could not make out what was embroidery and what blood-staining.

Mark Lane, the Chief, and Iles arrived at more or less the same time, Lane in a dark overcoat, Iles wearing a magnificently soft brown leather bomber jacket, brown slouch hat and crimson scarf loosely tied.

'This would be one of her Tambo trips, Col?' he asked.

'Appalling, appalling, Colin,' Lane said. 'You shouldn't be here. Francis Garland can handle it.'

'I don't expect Harpur can face them at home, sir,' Iles replied. 'Kids – they get intimations about these things, somehow. Sexual attack?'

'Her clothes seemed intact,' Harpur said.

'Skilled knifing?' Iles asked.

'As the hospital says, she's dead.'

'How many blows?'

'Three.'

'Yes, skilled. Apparently not theft. Col, perhaps one for me to look at in person? That make your flesh creep?'

'She was a lovely, inoffensive woman,' Lane said, 'and a wonderful wife and mother, I know. And so near Christmas.'

'Christmas survives, sir,' Iles replied. 'It's got a track record. Hit by some sort of professional. She ranged a bit, Col? Well, obviously. They do. But even more than was generally known? Into what?' The crimson scarf fluttered about his face and he did nothing to stop it, as if keen on the touch of raciness this gave. 'Many do like the full life these days, and all credit to them I say, sir,' he told Lane. 'Can they cope, though?' He waved a hand towards the spot where Megan had lain and the neat border of purchases.

'She would be travelling alone?' Lane asked.

'As far as Colin knows, sir,' Iles said.

'She would be travelling alone, Colin?'

'As far as I know, sir.'

'Tambo wouldn't ever come back with her?' Iles asked. 'But why should he?'

Lane said: 'When you say Tambo you mean—?'

'Yes. My predecessor as ACC here, sir. A *tendresse*. Before your time. He's some sort of Assistant Deputy Assistant or Deputy Assistant Deputy in the Met now. Leicester graduate, or possibly Oxford. Somewhere like that. Fine skin here and there. You could see how he might fool women. Megan loathed police, yet here she is tied up with two of them. Blood's such a tyrant. Thank God, I say myself, sir, wouldn't you?'

'Your poor daughters, Colin,' Lane replied. 'They were so very close to Megan.'

'Passably close, sir,' Iles said. The ACC tried not to agree with Lane too often, nor to disguise his contempt for him too often. Under Barton, Lane's predecessor, Iles had sometimes been able to act as Deputy, though still officially only an Assistant Chief. Lane kept him very much to Assistant. Iles noticed.

Chapter 5

Tambo had put her on the train. Well, nearly. He could not risk walking with her at that hour, when there were so few people about. It was conspicuous. Police patrolled London stations and he might be recognized, so he drove Megan to a spot from which they could almost see her platform. He was divorced, yes, but she was not, and it would do him no good to be discovered in an adulterous affair with the wife of another officer. They kissed in the car and she did this last stretch alone. He watched and she turned just before going out of sight. He waved but she did not, because it might direct attention. That was their drill, the sort of caginess you accepted in these situations. He had to take care of his job. Certainly it was understandable.

In her train seat now, as she thought of that walk from his car and replayed the moment, the face and moustache of the man in the next but one carriage suddenly surfaced in her memory, a kind of double-take. Had he been one of a scatter of people behind her and making for the train, perhaps also coming from a car or cab? She had not been giving much attention because there was no need, simply looking back to glimpse Tambo and say silently across the distance that it had all been lovely and great, despite those few evil moments. Gazing out into the blackness as her train rattled on, could she dig up now from a corner of her subconscious a face put there without her knowing it by a corner of her eye?

And what did it matter if she could? This man had obviously boarded the train – he was here, in view now – so why shouldn't he have been hurrying behind her? Jabbing her mind so it would rehash the scene, she visualized Tambo's car,

13

Tambo at the wound-down driver's window staring in her direction, waving hard, perhaps sentimentally leaning out as for an extra bit of closeness. Then she was alongside the festooned station Christmas tree high up alongside the Departures and Arrivals boards. She thought she recalled a group of three women, all with shopping, a man also with shopping and another man, carrying nothing, this man. It struck her that she did think of Tambo as staring *in her direction* – not at her but only in her direction. Had he suddenly spotted the man behind her, knew him somehow, was preoccupied by him? Did he mean some signal, some warning in the violent way he waved? Megan had turned on to her platform then, lost sight of Tambo, and hurried because of last-call whistles: she had lingered with Tambo in the car almost too long, trying to put things right. Both of them tried to put things right. They were a constructive pair.

The face in her recollection had now taken on clarity, or such clarity as she could manage from a carriage and a half away. And that was the point, wasn't it? Damned hindsight, nothing but. Of course: imposing this man's looks, the fellow traveller's looks, on to what had at first been only an uncertain, utterly vague half-memory of a figure behind her on the forecourt, dimmer then in her recall than the shape of the Christmas tree. In computer lingo there was something called ROM, a Read-Only Memory, meaning what was on a disc could not be added to. But she was adding to memory, wasn't she, fretting herself into a conviction that the two men were the same, and childishly overlaying that with menace? A minute ago she had not even been sure there was anyone at all behind her on the forecourt. Now, she had concocted threat, a scenario to endorse her stupid tension.

She was glad that from behind her somewhere in the long carriage she could hear voices, a man's and a woman's, the man talking very steadily, the woman occasionally saying, 'Yes, indeed', or 'Amusing.' Megan was not alone, and she took comfort. It was untypical of her to need such support, and she wanted to know why it had happened, this panic, this collapse into poisoned fancy. She turned from the window and glanced up the train again. He was still there, upright, motionless, perhaps gazing at her, perhaps gazing past her, perhaps gazing at nothing, but dozing. Again she felt that mixture of reactions. If his eyes were fixed on her, she would worry. If he was sleeping, fine. If he saw her but was not impressed enough to keep his eyes on her she would be hurt, a little. At least a little. It was one of the nice things a lover could do: make a woman think every man owed her attention, and that only fools or the undersexed refused it.

This was the moment when she decided she wanted Tambo and only Tambo. She was at sea, her feelings a jumble. She needed solidity, and he was it. Much of their short time together today she had spent telling him she could not leave Colin and the girls, at least not yet. They had had the same argument before, often. Today, though, it had been especially painful and harsh, and, walking from his car to the train, she wondered if irreparable things had been said. And so the attempt to send the long-distance message to his car that all would be well. Now, trying to spot home-stretch landmarks through the window, she realized she did not want this kind of life any more, craved certainty and recognition of matters as they were – knew she had to tell Colin it was finished and she must leave.

Perhaps she smiled minutely, at the tortuous, contrary ways by which she had reached this point. Up the train the man seemed to return the small smile. That scared her, and gratified her. But she did not want her smile misunderstood and turned away, pretending to check some items in her carrier bags. When she glanced back, he was unquestionably watching, definitely not asleep, eyes visible and interested.

Chapter 6

Iles lived and lasted by venom, of course, but would show occasional links with humanity. Harpur had seen that happen more than once, and even more than twice. It could be unsettling. As Francis Garland ran his widening ground search at the car park for a weapon and anything else, the Assistant Chief had said: 'I'll come home with you, Col. You'll need help breaking it to the children, and, clearly, you nor they would want Mark Lane there vulgarizing her death with unction, the dear man. Leave it to me. I'll head His Worthiness off.'

The Chief had withdrawn to his car and was sitting crouched forward a little over the wheel, the collar of his overcoat up, more or less concealing his features. 'In monkish prayer, would you say, Col?' Once, Lane was a great detective, but now promotion and Iles had started to undo him, in their notorious ways.

At home, the girls were getting themselves ready for school when Harpur and Iles arrived, and at once seemed to sense something bad from the two men's appearance and the fact that Megan remained missing. After a couple of seconds, Jill began to weep. At first she covered her face with her hands, then let them fall back and stood in the middle of the room, her eyes and mouth wide, the tears lumping up for a moment on her cheekbones before dropping to bounce from her lower lip and spray out in front. She tried to speak, to ask what had happened, but the words did not form.

Hazel stared at her, as if yearning to believe Jill was acting childishly, crying before she had been hurt, and yet fearing, knowing, her sister had it right. She turned from Jill and glanced at Harpur really studying his face now. Then she also began to weep, but lowered her head quickly towards her shoulder, so Harpur could not see her properly, and, he realized suddenly, especially so Iles could not see her properly. Harpur went quickly and put an arm around her. They both walked like that to Jill and he held her to him with his other arm. She pushed her face hard into his chest and he felt the warm damp of her tears soak through.

Iles, undoubtedly knowing pretty well what they thought of him, stayed near the door of the room and kept silent so far, fiddling with his gorgeous scarf, doing all he could to look unimperious. Hazel used to refer to him as 'the feral loony'. He would occasionally send them money presents via Harpur at their birthdays or Christmas but tell him to say they came from elsewhere.

'Is this some accident?' Hazel asked. Slowly, she detached herself from Harpur. She had become the elder sister, able to stand alone, entitled to a report, demanding things should be spelled out. Picking up a cushion from an armchair, she wiped her face with it, then wept again.

'No, not an accident,' Harpur replied.

'And she's dead?' Hazel said.

'Yes.'

'Oh, Mummy, Mummy,' Jill bellowed. 'Dad, you're saying murdered? Mummy? This is something to do with the dirty lives the two of you have? Had.'

Iles said: 'Whenever I spoke to your mother you two girls were uppermost in her mind.'

'*He* was supposed to be uppermost in her mind, and she in his,' Hazel replied. 'It's called marriage. Heard of that?' She rubbed her face with the cushion again and then threw it from her, back on to the chair. There was a time for grief, and it had gone. It had not, but Harpur admired the effort, would have expected it from her.

Iles said: 'Marriage? Yes, but things are subject to change.'

'Why?'

'Time's a villain.'

'What a prospect. Who's going to find who did it?' Hazel asked.

'Mr Iles,' Harpur said.

'That's something,' Hazel said.

'Thanks,' Iles replied.

'They haven't got a chance if it's him,' Hazel said.

'Thanks.'

'People need someone like you now and then. Like a lavatory brush.'

'Thanks, Hazel. It's called policing. Heard of that?'

Hazel took a few steps towards the door. Harpur thought she would take her sorrow to her room. Then she turned suddenly and went and touched Iles briefly on the arm of his bomber jacket. She was fifteen, almost womanly, Harpur saw, even in the school uniform. Iles remained still and silent, the red scarf in his hand trailing the floor. Hazel moved back and stood with Harpur and Jill again. Hazel wept once more, though without noise.

'Colin didn't want me to come. He thought this was private, and of course it *is*,' Iles told them. 'I didn't and still don't know what to say but I just thought it might be all right for someone who knows him well to be with him.' He spoke hesitantly to the girls, as though before a tribunal.

'Yes, it's all right,' Jill said. She glanced towards the cushion but then wiped her face on Harpur's shirt.

'There are gifts up there for you, but that's not the point,' Iles said. 'She never stopped thinking about you.'

'Up where?' Hazel replied.

'Where she was found,' Iles said.

'I don't ever want to know where,' Hazel replied.

'Right,' Iles said.

'Where was it?' Hazel asked. 'I won't have flowers left there, in a street or wherever – those corny "tributes" done on TV.'

'Some people mean well,' Iles replied.

'We thought she was going to leave,' Jill said.

Hazel said: 'No doubt of it.'

'Well, I suppose we all think of that now and again,' Iles replied. 'It's called marriage. Not so many actually do it. And, whatever she intended, you two would have been her supreme concern.'

'You've already said that. It doesn't make it any more true,' Hazel replied.

Jill said: 'He's doing his best, that's all, Hazel. Give him a chance.' She paused for a long moment, obviously gearing herself up. 'Is this her blood on you, Dad?'

'Well, yes,' Harpur replied.

'Colin did what he could,' Iles said.

'He always does what he can,' Hazel replied, 'but it's not always right or good enough.'

'I keep telling him that,' Iles said.

'So what about you?' Hazel replied.

'Hardly ever right or good,' Iles said, 'but it works now and then.'

'I heard,' Hazel said. 'You don't care about much, do you?'

'Not about much, I suppose.'

'Well, there's some breakfast left, Mr Iles,' Jill said. 'In view of you being up from an early hour. Cereal and quite warm tea I should think.'

'Sounds grand,' Iles replied, immediately sitting down at the table and filling one of the girls' bowls with muesli and milk for himself. He began to eat champingly with the used spoon. He poured himself some tea in Jill's cup. Harpur sat down with him but did not take anything.

'They won't let those grief counsellors loose on us, will they,' Hazel asked, 'encouraging full sorrow expression? We've done that. We're not children.'

'They're good people. Intelligent,' Iles said, sucking noisily at his tea. 'Grief's not just for children, is it? But not if you don't wish it.'

'Jill?' Hazel asked.

'Probably not,' Jill said.

'Perhaps for Dad. He's not as tough as he seems.'

'What I always tell him,' Iles remarked, 'and pompous with it.'

Chapter 7

Foraging in one of her carrier bags to avoid his eyes for a moment, Megan came upon the Irish linen embroidered tablecloth. The exquisite, pale colours of the work delighted her and so did the smooth, firm feel of the material. She drew comfort from handling it now, just as she drew comfort from the nice buzz of those decently modulated voices in another seat. These were matters right for First Class. The tablecloth almost made her smile again, and almost made her weep. It was something that told of good, festive family meals. The quality proclaimed continuance, durability. *This will look wonderful at Christmas dinner, but I won't be here. Not this Christmas, nor any after.* When she bought it the determination to leave had not formed in her head. But she reckoned that, even if it had, the pleasant habit of home building might have prevailed for the moment and she would probably still have taken it. She would leave it when she went. This was entirely a family item. Tambo would understand.

When she looked up the man was walking quite fast towards her – already out of his own carriage and into the one between. His eyes seemed to be on the carrier bag. Neither of her comforts – the voices, the tablecloth – could prevent dread and panic encompassing her again, very fast and more fiercely now. Her brain said, of course, that he might only be making for the lavatory, though he had probably passed one at the end of his own carriage. Perhaps it was occupied and he was on his way to the next. She could not believe it, though, would not believe it. He was on his way to her. And, even in her fear, she felt an absurd flutter of gratification. Had he found the distance between them intolerable and was coming to speak before it was too late and one or other of them left the train? It was notorious that such urgencies did hit people when they were put together by chance in travel.

She could see him better now, and the impression strengthened that she had noticed him before, yet perhaps not only behind her hurrying for the train. Her mind said it was somewhere else, also, but could not tell her where else. He was as young as she had thought – say twenty-four or five – but slighter, gaunter, more troubled, wilder. He had on what could be a genuine camel-hair navy overcoat with fur collar, a brightly white shirt and a brightly contrasting silver and red tie. The dark moustache looked wrong: too military for the face and the ensemble, as if from Gulf War newsreels. It was something about the way he walked – nimble, balanced, swift – that shoved her memory towards . . . But she could not say towards what, only knew that it was not only the station forecourt under the Christmas tree. And, as she rearranged her impressions of him, she realized he might be doing the same about her. Did men of twenty-four really feel an unstoppable urge to get on terms with women of thirty-six? From that distance, had he been able to tell how old she was? Would he see that now and feel cheated?

It was part this small spasm of injured vanity and part real fright which made her want to break whatever connection there might be between them. She found it intolerable to sit there docile, in plain view, simply waiting for him to get even closer. She stood and turned towards the luggage rack, where she had put two of her other carrier bags, and reached up to bring them down, as though wanting to go through the rest of her purchases. It helped her to present her back like that, displayed indifference to him, showed she was preoccupied with binding family things. Binding? And, as she was standing, her face and head visible now to the rest of the carriage, someone called, a woman: 'Why, Megan. How nice.' In a moment two people came from one of the seats and stood in the gangway alongside hers. 'Fancy not knowing you were there,' the woman said.

Megan glanced back towards the approaching man. He was almost at the door to this carriage and she was certain he would have come on, if it had not been for the sudden intervention of these two. Instead, he disappeared into the lavatory and the illuminated board changed from FREE to OCCUPIED. She felt relieved and disappointed. He might be as little as twenty-three or four. 'Coral,' she cried. 'And Roger. This is wonderful.'

'And you've been here all the time?' Roger said. 'All the way from London? What a pity – we could have joined up earlier. Shopping? Yes, us, too. We'll join you for the last bit?'

'Please. I heard talking – should have recognized the voices.'

'Well, a voice,' Coral said. 'Rog has been sounding off, rather.'

Megan resumed her seat and they joined her. In a while, she saw the illuminated board change again and watched the man return to his place. It was then, staring at his thinnish, tall frame, that her memory offered more geography. She suspected she might have glimpsed, half glimpsed, someone of that build, maybe that colouring, behind curtains at a window opposite the Careen Street flat today, conceivably watching. This would be before that possible encounter at the station. Was this more imagining, more hindsight? The figure in the window had scarcely been visible. But, if she was right, it would be an alarming coincidence. Chilling. This was someone who had turned up three times: the flat, station, here. Turned up only because she was present?

'Actually, we've been chewing at something that came up in the last literary discussion group at your house, Meg,' Roger said. 'Significance of common phrases – similes and so on.'

'Yes?' Megan replied. The man was back in his seat now, gazing towards her again.

Roger said: 'Take "as thick as two short planks". I mean, what does it actually mean, Megan? Have you considered? Why should short planks be thick? One could surely have short thin planks for certain delicate work or long thick ones.'

The train slowed and pulled in at Dobecross. A couple of people in the next carriage left, blocking her view for several minutes. When the train restarted the man's place was empty.

'Only another quarter of an hour,' Coral said.

Chapter 8

Naturally, people did leave flowers at the spot. The media had established a protocol for outdoor deaths. Harpur was with the two girls having supper cooked by Jill when it came up on television news, and there was a picture on an inside page of the *Daily Mail*, too, Harpur's paper. He could see the *Mail* was not perfect but had persisted as an identity matter, Megan loathing it so thoroughly. He might get something else delivered now, perhaps the *Telegraph*, or even *The Times*. And, of course, he would stop Megan's bloody *Guardian*: his daughters were already anti-police and needed no outside aid. But, not wanting to look callous, he would let things run as they were for a while.

There had been a small fall of snow, and in the television shots the flowers were part covered. They looked more as if discarded than placed.

Jill cried and then said: 'Well, *I* think it's very nice.'

'You would,' Hazel replied.

'Why not?' Jill asked.

'She didn't belong to them. What do they know? Sentiment.'

'She didn't belong to anyone, did she, Dad?'

'I don't mind people leaving flowers there,' Harpur replied.

'You're pathetically grateful for any sign of public friendliness,' Hazel said. 'Police always are. The thing to ask is why she had to be alone there at that time of night.'

'Mr Iles and Francis will find out all the circumstances,' Harpur replied.

'I don't mean that,' Hazel said.

'No, I know,' Harpur replied.

'Yes, I know,' Hazel said.

23

He was awoken at just after 1 a.m. that night by a noise in the house, possibly a door closing. For a while, he lay waiting for any repetition, wanting to locate the sound exactly. If there were people who would butcher Megan to settle scores, there might be people who would come to the house looking for him personally, or the girls. Was it a mistake to be in the telephone book? Two tabloids had produced identical head-lines: TOP COP'S WIFE IN REVENGE KILLING, not even a ques-tion mark. The Chief thought that with Megan's death chaos had come to the patch, and if to the patch to the nation. At that rank they were paid to think width. 'The filth is winning,' he had said.

'We'll see about that,' Iles replied, rubbing his knuckles on his teeth.

There was no further sound. Harpur left the bed and, in the darkness, peered about for anything that might do as a weapon. At Megan's insistence, they had preserved the original floral-tiled fireplace in this room, but no fire irons, though they had some downstairs. She kept a decoratively gaudy furled parasol there, souvenir of a holiday in Rimini, and he took this now. Standing in his Y-fronts and holding the parasol, he thought that maybe Lane had it right and police *were* under-equipped to deal with the current enemy. He opened the door quietly and stepped on to the landing. They would come so soon after her death, even before the funeral? For all they knew, the body was in the house. Himself, he loved breaking into other people's property on a pretext, looking secretly at their most personal stuff. Anyone trying it with him though would get a parasol. He edged forward a bit and listened over the stairwell, but still heard nothing.

First, he wanted to know the children were all right and gently opened Jill's door. At once, even without lights, he saw that her bed was empty, and he found Hazel's room the same. He went swiftly downstairs, still in darkness, and through all the ground floor, but found nobody. Returning to his bedroom, he replaced the parasol and dressed. He found his flashlight in the car and did a quick tour of the garden. Out there, the snow lay more or less undisturbed, except for footprints going out apparently to a holly bush and back. The marks might be Hazel's.

He drove towards the station car park and, after about half a mile, saw the two girls in school raincoats, gloves and rubber boots walking in that direction. They had made a rough wreath from the holly, which Hazel carried. Callipers were sticking from her pocket. When he drew up, they climbed into the back of the Granada. Nothing was said, except by Jill:

'This where you laid her out, Dad? Makes a change.'

He continued to the station and put the car as it had been the night he found Megan, the headlights on main. The tattered, half-buried flowers shown on television still lay there. The Astra had been on a space which had slightly raised brickwork on three sides to mark the perimeter and some of the flowers were supported by this minute wall. Both girls got out and went forward. Jill placed the wreath. They stood back, heads bowed, and kept very still. He left the car and went to join them. Clearing away some of the snow, he brisked up the flowers on the ground, in support of the central wreath. When crouched down like that in the glare he felt for a moment as he had that morning. Had there been enough grief, enough pain? He had done everything as right as it could be done, but was the grief there, the pain – as much as was fit? Had he believed she was too far from him?

Something else was triggered, too, as he bent over the spot. Just before lifting her, hadn't he been aware of an approaching vehicle, probably a car? It had been a long way off, but drawing closer, and then, as its headlights reached him, had seemed to stop suddenly, its engine still running. He thought that a few moments later, it went into gear again but turned away. The engine sound faded and had ended before he was at his own car with Megan. On that night, it had not seemed important, or not important enough, not a factor: maybe a taxi taking someone home, or a milkman. Now, though, more aware of the blaze of lights than he had been then, he wondered if whoever was in the car saw the beams from far off and for some reason withdrew. For *what* reason? The driver had been coming to find whether the job really had been done on Megan, and could not risk being identified?

'I grew to feel I might be wrong about the flowers, Dad,' Hazel said. 'Outnumbered – Jill, you and Desmond Iles. Stubbornness is stupid. The holly will stand up to it better – cars

25

churning about here – and seasonal. I'm not fully convinced, so I let Jill lay it. The Queen at the Cenotaph.'

'Iles will never find them. In a place like this, she was a sitting duck,' Jill said.

'All sorts of people will come forward from the train,' Harpur replied. 'Already have.'

'If she was going to leave anyway, did this hurt you all that much, Dad?' Hazel asked. She was clearly forcing herself to put the brutal, unavoidable questions. She sounded breathless, determined. 'Obviously, finding anyone in that state – it would upset you. But really tear you apart?'

'I've been trying to work that out,' Harpur said. They stood grouped around the spot, held by the lights, like film actors in a graveside scene, their shadows a big, unified blur.

'You went your own ways,' Jill remarked. 'That's what I say to friends who ask. Well, I have to tell them something.'

'Fair enough,' Harpur replied.

Hazel said, very hesitantly for her: 'But when you're married – what I mean, some would argue, you don't go your own ways when you're married. This is not what it's about. Some would say, Dad.'

'And yet with something powerful and good holding us, also,' Harpur replied.

'But *how* powerful?' Hazel asked. 'This question has to be put.'

'He means us,' Jill said.

'Yes,' Hazel replied.

'It's water under the bridge,' Jill said.

'Mr Iles was right when he said she thought primarily about you two,' Harpur replied.

'He came on strong about her,' Hazel said. 'Did he and Mum have something going at some stage?' She sounded ready to believe anything.

'No, no, he meant it,' Harpur said.

'She hated him,' Jill remarked. 'Iles likes them young. You, for instance.'

'Hating someone can be just the other side of the same coin, can't it, Dad?' Hazel replied.

'It can be.' He went to switch off the headlights before his

26

battery drained. It was best not to hurry the girls.

'The wreath gives a bit of class,' Hazel said. 'More traditional.'

'I think so,' Harpur replied.

'It would be wrong to let others put the flowers there and do nothing ourselves,' Jill said – 'as if she belonged to them. I mean, even if she didn't belong to us we still ought to do something.'

'She definitely did,' Harpur replied.

'I can't stand "definitely". It always means the opposite,' Jill said.

Chapter 9

In the train Megan, smiling and nodding, listened to Roger's lecture and thought: Arsehole, metaphor not simile. Roger genuinely depressed her. The Fortnightly, as her literary evenings were known, counted for much with Megan, but not if they made people talk like this. Those meetings were her attempt to assert a bit of herself at home and thin down the police ambience brought by Colin and Colin's mates and bosses. If these meetings amounted to nothing, or amounted to bloody Roger, it became even more plain that she must leave. She was wasting her time, her life. There was something in her which wanted to scream at him now that in fact she had another life, separate from the Fortnightly and Colin both, a fresh, thrilling vista, and that this was the last chance Roger would ever get to dump perceptions on her. There was even something in Megan which wanted now to reclaim contact with that stranger who had been diverted from speaking to her. Hadn't he? Surely. He was part of another, outside world – perhaps from London: fur collars were London, and that was where she had spotted him. He was a different age-group, perhaps dangerous, but what the hell, anything to escape Rog.

Since Tambo had landed his London job, she had begun yearning for the scope and excitement of the capital again. Brought up in Highgate, for the first few years of marriage she had cruelly missed metropolitan life. When she had the children, that ebbed for a while. Now, it was back, part because that's where Tambo was, part because London meant challenge, variety, range. Was this infantile? Probably there were Rogers in London, too, but they could be lost in the crowd. She realized it might seem gruesomely ironic that she was escaping from one cop to another. Easily explained, though. Police socialized with police. Married to Colin, how did she meet anyone else, except people like Roger – or not quite as bad as Roger, but on the way? In any case, Tambo wore his police identity more lightly than Colin. Tambo had interests: cinema, silver, horses, books. Perhaps the narrowness kept Colin where he was. It would not keep her there. She was entitled to better, had to be.

Roger said that idling away an afternoon in the summer while exam supervising at his college of higher education he had the idea for a poem called 'Invigilation', which he had now written and as luck would have it had with him. Some might deem it in poor taste, yet to his mind it contained a quite serious observation on the fat status given to that heavy item called Literature with a capital L. 'It's not too long, Megan. Shall I read it?'

'Of course you will,' Coral replied.

> One boy, one girl wore hats throughout
> The three-hour Shakespeare,
> But my thoughts were more on
> How, as far as I could tell,
> The whole two hundred of them
> Capped their farts this stressful
> Afternoon, not bothering one
> Another or us three. This was
> Primness of a type sometimes
> Neglected in the grandest work:
> 'I fart at thee' is on *The*
> *Alchemist*'s first page, and of course
> There's Toby Belch. Have we
> Made progress, then, and if so
> Is it manners or digestion/diet?
> Question Ten said: 'Time
> Has fitted Shakespeare with
> A holy robe of cultural
> Reverence which he would find
> Unwearable, Discuss.'
> And

Was this part of it – this
Docile *politesse*, this
Tidy bottling-up of nature
In the crouched and earnest
Frames?
'Answer one from the
Top section, all others from
Below. Display a range of
Reading, but not of *aide-memoires*
To mealtimes, especially from
Below. Remember you are tackling
Greatness, and deference is due.'

'I make no profound claim for it – I'm not Shakespeare,' Roger remarked, 'but I think there's a valid point, not so to speak just wind.'

The man who had sat watching from the other carriage might have left at Dobecross. Or had he simply gone to a different part of the train, perhaps looking for another woman travelling alone? That might be something of a relief, but it also peeved her a little, made her feel slighted – and feel grossly encumbered by these two. She had swung away almost completely from the fear that held her at first, and now found herself wanting to offer contact with this fur collar, declare she was not bound to provincials like Roger and Coral, was different from them, a risk-taker.

The only encouraging gesture she could think of was to go and use the lavatory after him, even if he did not know. At least she would escape Roger and Coral. She had to get rid of them. There was the appalling possibility they would be dependent on taxis when the train arrived, in which case she would have to offer them a lift and be a victim to more of Rog. Someone had told her about a Dutch student rebel novel, *I, Jan Creemer*, in which the anti-hero used to go to cafés, select an attractive woman, wait until she went to the bisex lavatory and then rush in afterwards, to get her warmth from the seat. This might not be quite like that, or not like it at all, but these days women could make their own initiatives, and she stood and walked to the end of the carriage.

'Don't hang as it were about,' Roger called. 'We're almost there.'

No message had been scrawled in steam on the looking glass or Biro'd on the next sheet of lavatory paper. Megan tidied herself up, refreshed her lipstick, as though the brilliant future were about to start instantly and needed to be adequately met. The train slowed. When she went back, Roger and Carol had returned to their seat. She took her time disembarking, to keep clear, but they made no attempt to waylay her. Perhaps Coral had notified him what a drag he was. Megan, two carrier bags in each hand, glanced about earnestly as the train drew out but saw nobody of special interest. Yes, she felt rather disappointed.

Chapter 10

Harpur and the girls, mainly the girls, did a bit of a tidy-up in the house because the Chief and his wife said they wanted to call before the day of the funeral. Lane was very thoroughly into caring and, while Iles had been able to keep him away at the time of Megan's death, Harpur knew a later visit must happen. The Chief was a good man, a necessary man at the top, though Megan and Jill always said too good to be police, and Iles always said too good to be any good, amounting to the same thing. The girls found him 'oozy', not hateful, and Hazel complained the sight of his lips gave her headaches. Just the same, they willingly cleaned the place up and Jill made Welsh cakes. They were both ready with talk topics to put the Chief and his wife, Sally, at ease.

'We wanted Mummy here, Mrs Lane, not left lonely in a funeral-home pigeonhole,' Hazel said. 'Dad wouldn't hear of it, though.'

'An understandable feeling in you, dear,' Mrs Lane replied, 'but there are arguments on both sides.'

'Mum's had enough loneliness. That car park in the early hours.'

'Hazel's doing her silly bit, Mrs Lane,' Jill replied. 'The dead can't be lonely or unlonely. But years ago it used to be normal to have the body in the house, especially working people, with neighbours paying respects etcetera. This is a good tradition. This makes death a community matter.'

'Oh, brave solidarity,' Hazel said. 'I wouldn't want neighbours in – Mrs Heston and other old bags staring at her, visualizing wounds.'

'She was well loved,' Mrs Lane said.

'I believe so,' Hazel replied. 'Desmond Iles is clever, yes, but I can't see where he'll even start his investigation. I mean, she had such an undiscoverable sort of life.'

'Both of them,' Jill said.

'Right,' Hazel replied.

'Well, I suppose we all have parts of our inner lives that are undiscoverable,' Sally Lane replied. 'This would be a valuable element in our respective identities.'

'She spread her identity around,' Hazel said. 'Will her, well, friend want to come to the funeral, Dad? He might feel he has a right. This would be terrible.'

It would be. Harpur felt hammered by the prospect of the funeral. Megan's parents were travelling down today, and he hoped Hazel and Jill would behave well to them in the circumstances. They were very well-intentioned Highgate doctors, and Megan, an only child, had injured them badly by marrying police.

'How do you see it, Mr Lane? The whys of this death,' Jill asked.

'Very early days yet, dear,' he replied.

'But what kind of motive?' Hazel asked. 'Not sex, not robbery, it seems. I saw one of the papers saying revenge, a hood family, maybe, getting at Dad for all the damage he's undoubtedly done to such people. This is far-fetched? You people planted that, trying to grab sympathy for police, the eternal quest?'

'Not just Mr Iles hunting this killer, but Francis Garland as well,' Sally Lane replied. 'These are wholly dedicated officers, I can assure you.'

Although the youngest one there, Jill had charge of the catering and rarely sat down. When she did it was alongside Harpur on a straight-backed chair under some sort of abstract painting Megan's parents had bought them for their tenth anniversary. Hazel and Jill were hostile to it, part because of itself – the lime dots and bulging, ochre balloons – part because of who had given it. Harpur, himself, did not mind the picture too much and had often defended it to his daughters.

'If these papers get a whiff of the kind of lives Mum and Dad went in for we're due for all kind of accurate muck on the front pages,' Hazel said. She lowered her head for a couple of moments over her cup and had a quiet, thorough cry. Jill, who was moving around with the teapot, set it down on the floor and went and stood by her sister's chair and put an arm around her neck. Hazel turned her head and wept for a while into the sleeve of Jill's sweater. After a few minutes, Hazel straightened up and Jill went back to the teapot. 'Honestly, Mrs Lane, you'd think neither of them had ever heard of hetero Aids,' Hazel said, wiping her eyes. 'I'm very sorry. They're a couple of sixties throwbacks. Pathetic.'

'We'll take great care about what gets to the Press,' Lane replied. He sounded more miserable about the possibilities than Hazel.

'Solitary in a car park at that hour,' Jill said, pouring for Harpur. 'What are reporters going to think? They'll dig for scandal. And then our school. The headmaster reads all the dumbo papers. That's about his mark. Like Dad.'

'We've a specialist officer who deals with the Press,' Lane replied. 'You mustn't worry.' Cowering a bit in his arm chair, the Chief reached out feebly for safer conversation: 'I do like this room. Obviously, a family centre in many respects, and yet with such a distinct flavour of Megan: the shelves full of much-used and much-loved books, not mere show bindings. These volumes went into the making of her. This is the room where the Fortnightlies were conducted, I think.'

'Megan was, indeed, a great book person,' Mrs Lane said, 'and I'm sure that when you children were smaller she would read to you. This is a wonderful introduction to literature – as an integral part of life. Books as *true* friends. It's a legacy you will never lose.'

'Jill's the reader,' Hazel replied. 'Even *Northanger* crummy *Abbey*, would you believe?'

'I'm glad it became every two weeks instead of four,' Jill said, 'because people called them her Monthlies.'

Harpur, gazing at the bookshelves, felt the pain of loss fiercely renew itself. The power of it surprised him. He had always admired Megan for running those meetings. They gave her something worthwhile that he could not, yet he had never felt excluded and would occasionally look in on a session.

Megan welcomed this. Last time, a week ago, they had been doing a feminist line which seemed to prove the mad woman in the attic in *Jane Eyre* was really the book's star, and not Orson Welles or Joan Fontaine. Women did have a damn rough time, on the whole. The Fortnightly people would see it as ironic that Megan earned foregrounding only now, in death. Tambo had come to a couple of her meetings, which was presumably how things started, or how they got into their stride. Harpur had nothing much against books, but rather a lot was made of them by some. The heat about Rushdie.

'Now, Christmas,' Sally Lane said. 'We won't badger you at this time, of course not, but Mark and I would love it if you would come to us for dinner.'

'Oh, absolutely,' Lane said.

'Well, Christmas plans were fluid, in case she wasn't here for it, anyway,' Hazel replied. 'I mean, in case she went, which seemed probable to all of us. But thank you very much. Garland won't get a look in on these inquiries, will he? Not with Iles around. Iles is always trying to squash him. Naturally. Everyone, but especially Garland. Naturally. That's to do with Sarah, Iles's wife, isn't it? So, really, we depend on one man to find what happened to Mum – certainly ace in his poisonous way, but still only one.'

'Francis Garland doesn't let himself get squashed,' Harpur replied. 'An ego.'

'So will you be spilling to Ilesy all you know about Mum's life, Dad?' Hazel asked. 'You can really score off her now, can't you?'

'He's not like that,' Jill replied.

Sally Lane said: 'Whatever your mother may have done in her private life, she—'

'Mrs Lane – not meaning to be in any way rude, but you're not going to tell us she had Hazel and me in mind all the time, are you? Iles really flogged that one.'

'Desmond has a very warm, well-meaning side,' Lane replied.

'I've heard that,' Hazel said.

Harpur had always liked having the Chief in his house. He radiated family virtues and gave a feeling of solidity, of good

35

ordinariness, not just his clothes but the intelligent, cheerful interest he took in workaday domestic detail. Sally helped. They almost always enabled Harpur to believe, for a while, at any rate, that decent, normal life went powerfully on, despite everything: despite, even, Lane's frequent, headlong falls into paralysed despair, when Iles would have to drop his own work and hurriedly take over. The ACC always did it without any more resentment than he already felt for Lane. Holding his Welsh cake in the air, the Chief said now: 'Anyone can see you will still be well looked after, Colin.'

Chapter 11

Bizarre, but coming over the station footbridge on her way down into the deep dark of the car park's approach lane, Megan had found herself thinking about a painting her parents gave them one anniversary. Called *Associations 3*, it was a horribly lurid abstract which Colin, all credit to him, always pretended to like. Desmond Iles had referred to its 'devastating courage' and 'contempt for mere draughtsmanship', and this hurt. Iles had also wondered aloud whether there were *Associations 1* and *2*, 'mere workings towards this final statement. If, Megan, Colin, it *is* final. Might there be *Associations 4* through to, say, *17*?'

Megan's own proposal had been that they should keep the work in a cupboard under the stairs until her parents visited and then hang it for the duration. Colin would not allow this, though, arguing it would make her parents look foolish in the eyes of the children. He could be painfully considerate. Her view was that if her mother and father bought such an object they deserved to look foolish, but he saw this as disrespectful and callous, so the picture had a permanent spot on a main wall, visible to everybody. Of course, the thing about Colin was he found one abstract painting as gross as any other, and *Associations 3* gave him none of the special offence it did to Megan and the girls. Crossing the bridge with her carrier bags, Megan was wondering whether she would have to take it with her when she left. Her parents might expect that and, with their opinion of Colin and police generally, would never believe he insisted on keeping it, or any other artistic item.

She could see why she let herself get obsessed now by this dud painting: to dodge the question of what was going to happen to the children – to go on dodging it. And to go on dodging something else: the shame she felt at growing so stupidly excited about Monsieur Fur Collar in the train. Good Lord, she had just spent a day with her lover, had been rehearsing ways to say goodbye for good to her husband, and she could still struggle to get the attention of another man, quite possibly a dangerous man. Sickening, girlish vanity. Was he really the one who had been in the window opposite Tambo's place and at the station? Thank God he left at Dobecross. Thank God, too, she could just make out Roger and Coral ahead, making for their car. They would not need a lift.

It was a laughable fudge to call it Tambo's place. This was a large and beautiful flat on the ground floor of a Mayfair block, lent to him whenever he needed it by some friend. Or what he called a friend. She did not greatly like the idea of a grace and favour flat. The arrangement reminded her too much of that Billy Wilder film about sleazy sex and near suicide, *The Apartment*. Tambo was vague on who lent it, and she hated that aspect, too. When they wanted, police could be supreme at vagueness, something that unnerved and enraged her in Colin. In the company of high-rank police – during ordinary, affable conversation with them – you might suddenly get glimpses of another shadowed, worrying, foully violent world. And while you were trying to adjust and cope, the curtains would suddenly shut totally, blanking it off again. Who from such a *de luxe* setting as 26A Careen Street would know Tambo so well? Oh, God, why couldn't she get close to some man who was not police? Mummy and Daddy would regard her as mad twice.

In the car park, Coral and Roger's Orion approached and passed, and she raised her carrier bags into the headlight glare as salute. Despite Rog, Coral always seemed reasonably happy. Perhaps she, too, had something else going. Six or seven people from the train were at their cars and revving up. There was a little snow in the wind and the occasional flake settled gently on her eyelids, neck and cheek, like being caressed in happy welcome. The car park lights had been vandalized, or British Rail was economizing. Perhaps she need not have hung back quite so far from the rest, but the carriers had slowed her, too. All the other women sported a man to share the load.

Just the same, she stayed thrilled with what she had bought, especially the sparkling Irish linen tablecloth, even if she did have to leave it when she went. Tambo had shopped with her. They thought they could risk that, and wanted all the time together they could get. A little sadly, he had watched her exult when the assistant part unrolled the tablecloth for inspection. 'Still home-building, then?' he muttered.

She had picked up the word. 'Come on, let's go home right away.' Home today was the gorgeous, spruce, unhomely flat, with the complimentary Taittinger in the fridge. They had intended seeing the film *JFK*, but that could wait. It had already waited nearly thirty years. When they first started using this flat she wondered who saw to the sheets and so on afterwards, but you grew used to accepting without too many questions what was offered.

At the Astra she set down the carriers on the white ground and looked for her handbag and keys.

Chapter 12

Tambo kept the two keys for the Mayfair flat in a zipped pocket of his wallet and he had been bringing out the one for the street door when Megan half noticed movement behind heavy net curtains of a first-storey window opposite, and she had the impression – not much more than that – of a man giving them some attention. Well, at first she thought possibly giving her, specifically, some attention, and therefore did not mention it to Tambo. He was preoccupied with the key and door, and seemed unaware of the observer, if he was that. She experienced a tumbled mix of reactions.

First, there was the carrier bags. What did these do for her appearance? Would she strike anyone watching as boringly domesticated? They were good carrier bags, including two from Harrods, so they might make her come across as someone with bright taste and money, an impression the flat block would endorse. But perhaps come across, too, as bourgeois and dully satisfied with her life? Entrance to the flat block was via a small railed front garden or area, leading to a wide and heavy front door, with a collection of black security voice boxes to one side. She and Tambo must look like a loaded couple returning gloatingly to their fastness with a morning's classy Christmas spoils.

Of course, all that was absurd. The man across the street had his fastness, too, didn't he? And, in any case, this was not domesticity for Megan and Tambo. They were steamingly illicit and here for love in the afternoon, and to hell with *JFK*. These damn carrier bags were part of a pretext, that was all: official reason for coming to London. Irony encompassed the situation, but he was not to know that. Normally, she would be appallingly tense when approaching this front door, in case she and Tambo should look like the adulterous couple they were, set on getting between the provided sheets, which they also were. Today, though, for these few silly seconds she felt anxious the two of them would seem monstrously married and steady, a banal pair from higher suburbia. The house opposite had a small parking square in front and a yellow VW Beetle stood there. It made her think the man might be young, a little racy, metropolitan smart. She felt gratified by his interest.

And then, in the jumbled, anarchic way her memory operated sometimes – perhaps the way most people's memory operated – she had the sudden notion that this bloody VW might have been behind their taxi at some earlier point in the day, during the shopping. She thought she had perhaps heard it rasping near them in Beetle style. She had not looked back, but the sound was very distinctive. As Tambo opened the door, she wondered at the same moment whether this watcher was interested not just in her but in both of them, possibly, even, in Tambo only. This would make a tailing VW more credible.

Immediately, she had one of those rushes of rage she often experienced with Colin, too, when made suddenly conscious of that crude and secret and hazardous world he lived in for most of his time, and kept her out of. God, police: their games, their grim privacies. She had fancifully tried to read into that little shift of the curtain opposite signs of healthy big city admiration for her – and probably created it. Christ, so feeble-minded, Christ, so humiliating, Christ, at what age did a woman ditch such instant dreams? The donated champagne came out of the fridge and she took a big glass, and then another. She needed something to get her ego up from the floor. Taittinger would do that or may I call you Payola? She thought she heard the VW chug away, but did not go to the window to look. She was here to make it up to Tambo for the cold infidelity of the tablecloth.

'I love the way we shut that door and are sealed off for hours and hours, undiscoverable,' she said. 'This place – well, it's a wonderful kindness of someone.'

'It would most likely stand empty, otherwise. He owns a few in this street, bought now prices are right down.'

'A few? Wow – even when they're so-called cheap. This is someone—?'

'Who wishes me well and wishes you well, Megan, just hearing what I say about you.'

She sat down on one of the sofas hugging her drink and he poured both of them a little more and joined her.

'When you say "sealed off", Meg – I'm not just a series of nice episodes in your life, am I? The trip to London and all its happinesses once every few weeks, then back to real life at home?'

'This is real life, too. I think of this place as a kind of home as well, believe me.'

'Kind of.'

Chapter 13

Lying on the ground alongside her car's back wheel, there were moments when Megan had some good bits of lucidity. Consciousness came and went and, in the patches when she had it, she knew where she was and what had happened, what the cold square of wetness from her chest to her midriff was, and knew also that a spell of clarity was this only, a spell, and that soon she would slip into blackout again, and that dozing in snow was perilous, ask Captain Oates.

During the stretches when her mind was sharp, she also saw that there were middle-ground stages between this state and total shut-off. In this half-and-half condition, she would imagine she was fine and safe, protected on one side by the high, dark wall of her car and on the other by a lower but comforting series of ramparts made by her carrier bag contents, placed in a line near. The word 'fastness' that came to her outside the borrowed passion nest seemed dead right once more. This was lunatic but she recognized it as lunatic only in those short and shortening periods when her brain was doing full duty. And, when she did recognize it, the realization chilled her more than the snow or the blood under her clothes because she knew it meant she was hallucinating and probably on the way out. In one of those *compos mentis* remissions she noticed that not all the gifts were nicely stacked: the end of the tablecloth had unfurled and was being flipped by the wind against the front of the Astra. At some stage it must have dragged across her or she across it and was streaked with blood.

Also in her clear times she saw she must stand, get clear of this fucking fastness by pulling herself upright against the tyre and the bodywork of the Astra, eventually to prop herself and steady herself with elbows spread on its roof, quitting the deadly, stained ground. Her intelligence offered Megan this as a workable procedure, but her body would not have it and failed to move. Not totally: she could put out her right hand, lifting it from the rib-cage place where she been using her gloved fingers, as if to keep herself together through her coat and suit. And she could take hold of the tyre, get a kind of grip on the top of it, under the mudguard. Her careful plan was to utilize the support of this tyre to help her get to sitting first and, afterwards, a slow controlled swing on to her knees, perhaps by then with two hands clasping the tyre, real solidity. Subsequently, having rested, she would transfer her hands to the side of the Astra, palms pressed to it, taking some of her weight as she gradually straightened from her knees, a kind of abseiling, but going up, not down. This seemed an entirely feasible, mechanically efficient operation.

It worried her that she would be removing her hands from positions where they could press down and help her plug her wounds with clothing, yet the reality was, surely, that they could do nothing much, and *had* done nothing much in that line, and would be better used for climbing. She had taught the children what she had been taught by her own parents: to break a tough problem into items and knock them off piece-meal. This would be the technique for getting to her feet here.

Her hands and arms and the rest would not do it, though. She clutched the tyre with her fingers and struggled to tug herself for starters into that sitting position, but there was next to no strength in her hands or arms or anywhere else. It had bubbled out of her and still bubbled out of her. The effort in getting her hand to the tyre and in pulling at it made her gasp and brought the beginnings of a cloud over her brain once more. She lay back, returned her hand to its position on her chest. It was not all that bad here, surely, a kind of small, protected area, a keep, a fastness, bounded on one side by the rearing walls of the Astra and on the other by stacked London purchases, like defence mounds on the First War front. There was a song her father used to sing, he having learned it from *his* father, who had been at Ypres: 'If you want the sergeant-major, I know where he is, He's down in the deep dugout.' This little enclosure was her deep dugout. She could no longer be reached or hurt.

When she awoke again and her mind climbed out of this farcical pit she wondered about the practicalities of yelling. The practicalities, she saw, came under two headings: first, was she capable of yelling; and, second, would anyone hear? She gave it a try and some sound did issue, though feeble. She formed her larynx as for a scream and what came out could be just about reckoned a scream, but not one to take the world by storm. A little way outside the station, a couple of diesel engines shunted freight trucks, and this did signify there were people about despite the hour. Railways never slept. The noise of the operations swamped anything she could produce, though. This was a town rail station and there ought to be folk passing near, surely – maybe vandals or thieves doing the car park, or patrolling police trying to stop vandals or thieves doing the car park. In time someone might hear her dwindling squeak. How much time did she have? Why hadn't the thieves come and stolen her purchases already? She lay waiting for the shunting to pause and when it did raised her head as much as she could and let go another scream/whimper.

Would Colin come looking eventually? How long was eventually? It would be a tricky decision for him, supposing he was at home himself and aware how late she was. They did not poke about in each other's private lives. It was an understanding that had built itself imperceptibly, tact and silence gradually expanding. Sad, in a way. The children reckoned that marrieds should not have lives private from each other. They went for the traditional, and nothing wrong with that, except it had ceased to work for her and Colin. He would not wish to be seen policing her life or acting possessive, because that's not how it was any longer, and he would fear laying his own life open to the same. She managed to get her head a little way up off the ground again, not as high as last time, but not bad, and tried once more to cry out. At virtually the same moment the shunting, which had been on stop, resumed with a great clattering, stuttering rush. She sank back down and felt the shock of new snow under her chin. But it was not all that bad here, surely, a kind of small, protected area, a keep, a fastness, bounded on one side by the rearing walls of the Astra and on the other by stacked London purchases, like defence mounds on the First War front. There was a song her father used to sing, he having learned it from *his* father, who had been at Ypres: 'If you want the sergeant-major, I know where he is, He's down in the deep dugout.' This little enclosure was her deep dugout. She could no longer be reached or hurt.

Hadn't these notions already run through her head, though?

Chapter 14

The day before the funeral, Hazel disappeared. Harpur was doing midday dinner, a grossly onioned corned beef hash, which both girls usually went for all right, but Hazel did not turn up. He and Jill waited until 2.30 and then ate without her, though not much. Jill swore she had no idea where her sister might be, but they were both very fine liars and had spent a lot of time with one of his books on interrogation techniques, counter-techniques and the counters to the counters and so on. He went up and had a look at Hazel's room. Her black Antarctica anorak was missing and so were a pair of training shoes and probably some cord trousers. Everything else looked normal, so she meant to come back? It was not a real search. Hazel was fifteen and entitled to her privacies.

Downstairs he said: 'When did you last see her, Jill?'

'Oh, come on, Dad— When did you last see your sister?'

'When did you?'

'Breakfast?'

'It's important. I need to know if she's gone voluntarily, don't I? Are we—?'

'Targeted? Don't get melodramatic.'

'No.'

'Of course it's voluntary.'

'She said she was going?'

'I've told you, she said nothing. She's fifteen, for Heaven's sake.'

'That's right.'

'She's going to consult me?'

'Should I report it?'

'What? She missed a corned beef dinner?'

You could hardly get heavy with a kid of thirteen at a time of grief, for God's sake.

Although Hazel acted tough, as they both acted tough, she was the one more likely to fall to pieces, and he drove back out to the station car park, in case she was bitten by a pilgrimage mode. It was afternoon and all the spaces were taken. The snow had gone. A bright new Daimler stood where Megan had lain, bits of a couple of the flowers sticking out from under its offside wheel. The holly wreath might be intact and obscured by the car. As far as he could see at a quick examination of the bodywork, tyres, wipers, mirrors and lights, the Daimler had not been vandalized, and when he asked in the ticket office the couple of clerks said they had noticed no girl of Hazel's age hanging about there today. They recognized Harpur and were prepared to treat him with real kindness, although polite, in view of what one of them called 'this terrible tragedy on our ground'. They promised to keep an eye.

Returning to the Daimler, he thought of leaving some good etchings in the paintwork himself, now it was almost dark. Those clerks might put two and two together, though, if there were complaints. In the police, you had to think responsibly, even on personal matters. He did get to the front of the car and saw the wreath was flat. That probably meant Hazel had not been here, or perhaps was here before the Daimler. He stood the wreath up against the little dividing wall and did what he could for the flowers.

When he returned to the house, Megan's parents had arrived and Jill was entertaining them with tea and the left-over hash and left-over Welsh cakes. They both looked pretty bad, and he hoped Jill had been soft-pedalling. Despite everything, Harpur liked his in-laws. They ran very decent lives in their Highgate medical practice, never ignoring a call-out, though well into their sixties, and using no locums. They had the attitudes of their class and upbringing, attitudes which had helped keep the middle-class end of the Labour Party more or less afloat for decades, and did all they could, short of compromising themselves, to treat Harpur with tolerance, even affection. It could have been so much worse: Megan's mother had a brother and sister-in-law who were full Hampstead Fabians. Frequently, Harpur argued with his daughters about

48

their grandparents, trying to fathom the girls' enmity and moderate it. It went back to when they were small, much predating the abstract painting.

'Jill tells us you actually found Megan yourself, Colin,' Daphne Pointer said. 'We know so little – your terrible phone call, and then what we read in the papers. Perhaps even more terrible.'

'They don't care what they say, Daphne,' Harpur replied.

'London?' she said. 'A day in London, and yet she was not in touch with us, not even a bell? It seems so unlike Megan. She was familial.'

'Really tearing around the shops, you see,' he replied. 'Only a day trip.'

'Plus she likes to, liked to, take in some really meaty play or movie that might not come here,' Jill said.

Daphne's nice face lightened for a second. She was sharp-featured but benign looking, with brown eyes which were sad now though animated, and skin as clear as Jill's 'Yes, Megan liked to take a wider view. Clifford instilled that, didn't you dear? From the start.'

Clifford said: 'So she went to London regularly, Colin? Always alone?'

'I'm tied. The children at school.'

'We would have loved to meet her – lunch, as brief as she liked.' Daphne worked her lips. 'Never a contact.'

'Please, don't be hurt,' Harpur replied. 'She did value time alone now and then. We all grew to accept that.'

Jill said: 'She used to tell Hazel and I—'

'Hazel and me,' Clifford said.

'Well, yes.' Jill replied. 'She said it didn't mean she could not be bothered with us, not at all. As Dad says, we fully accepted this. This was her nature. It would be the same as far as you were concerned.'

'Where *is* dear Hazel?' Daphne asked.

Clifford said: 'But you wouldn't have been going to meet Megan that night, obviously, Colin. She had her own car waiting.' His face was long and sallow, as mild as his wife's, and in normal times full of optimism and enduring vim. Highgate was going to miss these two eventually.

'She was very late,' Harpur replied.

49

'You were anxious?' Daphne asked. 'These awful revenge suggestions in the papers.'

'Puzzled more than anxious. Something wrong with her car?'

Clifford said strongly: 'I want to be very clear, Colin, that if this were, is, an attack on Megan as a way of getting back at you, we would not deem you or your job to be in any way blameworthy as the cause of our daughter's murder. Quite regardless.'

'Well, thanks, Cliff.'

Pointer glanced at Jill. 'Our view is that if your work carries risks, which it surely does, then the family cannot but be involved. Megan, we are sure, was aware of that when you married.'

'In those days I was looking at bicycle thefts.'

'None the less,' Clifford replied.

'She would want to be a full part of your life,' Daphne said. 'Regardless.'

'Thanks, Daphne, Cliff. We think a simple mugging.'

'Yet nothing taken?' Daphne replied.

'Who'd take some Paddy tablecloth or that wanker's tie he's got on?' Jill asked.

'Yours is a job that unquestionably has to be done, Colin,' Clifford said generously, 'and we should all acknowledge that and try to understand the conditions under which it must be done.'

Daphne asked: 'Did she speak? Do you think she recognized you, Colin? I hope so.'

'Yes, she clearly spoke my name,' Harpur replied. 'And I told her she should hold on and that I would get her to hospital and she'd be all right. She replied: "I know it, I know it, Col." '

Jill stood and began to clear away the dishes, though without undue noise, and went into the kitchen.

'She thought so much of you, Colin,' Daphne said. 'Perhaps that night in the car park she knew her condition was hopeless. Megan was not one to fool herself, and she was very clever. But I like this assertion of hope and mutuality to the end. There were times when one worried about the two of you. How things were going? This striking out alone by her, and perhaps by you, too, if I may say. One doesn't know. Ultimately, though, no rift.'

'Darling, we brought her up to be independent,' Clifford said. 'Her Cambridge tutor said she'd never encountered such independence coupled with width of reading and knowledge in an undergraduate.'

Daphne said: 'Yes, I know, but—'

Jill came back in and sat down. 'Shall you see Mummy before the fire? Well, obviously not afterwards.'

'I think so,' Clifford replied.

'For myself, I'm not sure,' Jill said. 'I certainly don't say that what's there now in a box at the funeral parlour – parlour, I mean! – is unrelated to Mummy in any way. Of course it is. On the other hand, this is no *person*. Saying farewell and all that is just make-believe. Maybe necessary make-believe.'

'I don't mind some necessary make-believe,' Harpur replied.

'I know,' Jill said. 'So do juries know.'

'And how does Hazel feel about it?' Daphne replied.

'Seeing Mum?' Jill said. She shrugged. 'Who's ever sure of what that one feels and thinks? You know that word "enigmatic" at all, which I found lately?'

'Where *is* Hazel?' Clifford replied.

'She'll show soon, I expect,' Jill said. 'She likes to distance herself, make out she's scarce?'

'And, Colin, when you were actually carrying Megan to the car – Jilly tells us you did that – did she speak then?' Daphne asked.

'Only my name.'

'Jill,' Jill said. 'Nobody calls me Jilly.'

'Over and over, Colin?' Daphne replied.

'More than once,' Harpur said. 'By then she was very weak.'

Jill said: 'Not even sure about going to the funeral. Rigmarole? I know to show respect and experts say let your grief hang out and that. But I wonder.'

Harpur sat up alone and at just after 2 a.m. heard a car. After a few minutes, Hazel came in with Iles. He had on his long large-check Scottish moors overcoat and a brown, brilliantly sharp trilby, the sort of thing you saw on horse trainers when Ascot was televised. 'We met in Harrods, Col,' he said. 'Quizzing the same people.'

Hazel pulled off her anorak and wrinkled her nose. 'That their car outside?'

'They're asleep,' Harpur replied.

'I wanted to go over Mummy's route, that's all, Dad. The names on the carrier bags. Just to be sort of with her before . . . well, in these few days. I know it's stupid. But thinking of her all alone. She wasn't, of course, not in the shops and wherever else up there.'

'Naturally, I'm looking at the carrier bag trail, too,' Iles said. 'Then we returned on the train together. But Hazel didn't want me in the same carriage. Verisimilitude? Concerned to be like her mother, alone. I sat a couple of carriages away, Col, keeping an eye. She's fine.'

'It's all right, Dad. I know he goes for young stuff sometimes, but Mr Iles didn't try the least thing. Two shops said a smartly dressed man with her, over six feet. Another cop? What you could expect.'

'People are entitled to a life apart, perhaps,' Iles remarked.

'A death apart?' she replied.

'Hazel, that's merely flip,' Iles said.

'I know, I know. All deaths are apart.' She began to cry and Iles moved to her and put his arms around her very gently. To Harpur, it looked avuncular, even fatherly, and probably all right. Hazel did not recoil or hiss.

'Where did the rail fare come from?' Harpur asked.

'I had some,' Hazel replied.

'A lot. You went First? Verisimilitude? Jill subsidized? This was a joint thing?'

'Jill knows nothing.'

'You've got a solid team here, Col,' Iles said. 'She wanted ten minutes by herself in the car park when we arrived. I stayed clear.'

'Honestly, he did, Dad.' She disengaged herself decisively from Iles. 'People are being nice, reverencing the spot, leaving it free. The wreath was standing undisturbed when I looked just now.'

'People are grand,' Harpur replied.

'Oh, no, Harpur,' Iles said. 'Don't slip into that slimy myth or we'll never beat them.' On his way out the ACC handed Harpur a couple of crumpled bits of paper which, after a moment, he saw were fifty notes. 'Smuggle it back to her, them, somehow, for the fare, Col. Say you're paying. Obviously, they'd never take it from me.'

'This isn't at all necessary, sir.'

'Of course it isn't fucking necessary, Harpur,' he remarked, making for his car.

Chapter 15

In the flat with Tambo, the Beetle and the imagined observer forgotten, she devoted herself to love. It was probably crazy, in any case, to connect that VW with a sound she had heard, might have heard, this morning. Coming here now, early, and ditching *JFK* was an impulse, surrender to a surge of feeling and appetite which must, must put everything all right again and make Tambo see he was the only one who counted for her. The sex with him was and had to be ungovernable, raw, noisy of course, thought-free. It had to tell their tale, acting out and spelling out the power of what forced them together, the inevitability. Anxieties, fears, doubts had no part, would be a kind of betrayal. The Taittinger helped plenty.

Sometimes, in the frenzy, and almost always afterwards, she would wonder whether the loving was like that because illicit and rare, and in a dubious, exciting locale, such as this flat. How would she and Tambo be if they were together as a norm on their own sheets? It was this thinking that made her fend off today – fend off again today – his questions about when she would leave and set up with him. They were dressing, both hungry now, wondering where to eat. Tambo was a long time divorced, and a long time in need of a steady and unsecret relationship: in need of marriage, something to go with the big job. Megan could not tell whether it would work. How often could you switch on something like what both of them had switched on just now, and especially herself?

'I'm a bit on the side,' Tambo said. 'You're Liberated Woman.'

Chapter 16

Both Harpur's daughters' boyfriends arrived at Arthur Street in the morning, Darren in a suit and darkish shirt and looking sombre. Harpur realized after a while that they meant to come to the funeral and he could not have felt more grateful. They would have often met Megan, possibly liked her. Perhaps Jill was only bating her grandparents when she said she might not attend. These two lads had been on the scene for quite a while, especially Jill's Darren, and, by inviting them, the girls probably aimed at a public statement backing sexual loyalty.

Hazel did a great all-round breakfast, including chips, and the seven of them sat down with the food and two pots of tea at the big kitchen table – the four youngsters, Megan's parents and Harpur. Probably this was the table Megan had in mind for the Irish tablecloth, but it was with the investigation at present. The girls apparently meant to go to the funeral in their ordinary non-school clothes. Harpur would have liked some obvious sign of mourning, but had said nothing. Mrs Pointer had a grey top coat with her. Clifford had a black leather jacket and black leather overcoat and Harpur was in a dark suit and would wear a navy raincoat and black silk scarf. He wanted the day over.

Soon after they had started eating, Sarah and Desmond Iles appeared, Iles carrying champagne and orange juice in a cold box for Buck's Fizz. Dapper, slight, grey and hardly big enough for the police, Iles had on his dark blue ACC's dress uniform and looked warlike and brilliant. 'I always think it's *before* a funeral that people need the sustenance and so on,' he told Megan's parents. 'The baked meats after are all very well, but by then the damage has been done.'

'There'll be the baked meats afterwards, anyway,' Jill replied. She stood up, ready to cook more chips, black pudding, tomatoes and eggs for these two, but Iles said she must not interrupt her breakfast and went to the stove himself. He ignored the wrap-around purple and gold *Munchy Man* apron offered by Harpur.

'This commissionaire doubles as chef,' Sarah said. She forced the champagne corks and made drinks for everyone.

'Insignia is expected at a funeral,' Jill replied.

'Could you two wear something black?' Harpur asked.

At once he saw that the question might be an error, and Jill looked as though she would break down again. But then he watched her deliberately toughen, turn almost brutal, obviously determined not to collapse in front of the Pointers. 'You know about DNA tests, do you, Mr Iles?' she asked.

'All that's very much in hand,' the ACC replied.

'I feel Megan would be pleased to see us assembled and well provided for like this,' Clifford said.

'Well, we'll eat whether or not,' Hazel replied.

'She never thought much of me,' Iles said.

'Right,' Jill replied.

'Stow the self-pity till you've finished, Des,' Sarah said. 'Tears make eggs runny.' She was in dark green – a suit and three-quarter-length coat – and wore a black beret-style hat. Was she beginning to age a bit around the neck and under her eyes? Harpur grieved to see that happen. She had been so glorious.

Clifford Pointer stood with his glass of Buck's Fizz, the long, grey face sad but brave. 'May I offer a toast, the toast I'm sure Megan would wish for. Certainly she would not expect capitulation to grief. Simply then, To Those Who Follow On.'

Nobody took any notice, except Darren and Daphne. Darren half rose from the table and then, catching Jill's eye, sat back and took up his knife and fork again. Daphne grunted into her glass what might have been, 'To Those Who Follow On.' Clifford resumed his chair.

'Christmas,' Daphne Pointer said. 'We'd very much like you and the children to come to us, Colin, wouldn't we, Clifford?'

'Rather.'

'I heard you're already invited,' Sarah said. 'The Lanes? As a matter of fact, Des wanted you to come to us. Me too, naturally.'

'That sounds good,' Jill replied.

'But if you've already been asked?' Daphne said.

'Asked only,' Jill replied. 'We stalled. Christmas with the Lanes? Lord.'

'But the Chief Constable,' Clifford said.

'Or at Highgate: Christmas as a real family occasion,' Daphne said.

'What do you do at Yule?' Hazel asked Sarah.

'A video, *Basic Instinct*, or something meatier,' Iles said, dishing up at the stove. 'Charades based entirely on Chaucer. You know, they couldn't get anywhere near my *Parliament of Fowls* last year.' He put down the fish slice and a plate for a moment and did an imitation of Big Ben and then of a squad of lovable chickens. 'Afterwards, the Insults Game – seeing who gets hurt the easiest and goes ape.'

'Never Desmond,' Sarah said.

'Heard them all before, from my mother's knee.'

'Great,' Jill replied. 'Can Darren and Scott come?'

'Open invitation, obviously,' Iles said.

'Great,' Jill said.

'I don't know,' Scott replied. 'My mother frets about me being associated with police. What she calls it is "tarred with their brush".'

'So wise,' Sarah said. 'I wish *my* mother had warned *me*.'

'Why I couldn't wear a suit today,' Scott said. 'I had to slip out. She definitely wouldn't want me to go to the funeral, in case I'm targeted.'

'Turd, this isn't police,' Hazel sobbed at him. 'It's *my* mother. You're seventeen, not a babe.'

'She's scared,' Scott said. 'Reprisals. That's my father's word. And "courting trouble" he thinks.'

'What did Mum do up there all that time?' Jill said, willing things away from sorrow and back to the nitty-gritty. 'That's the puzzle, isn't it, Mr Iles? Hazel's gone over the ground, plus we've researched with street maps and a stop-watch. All those carrier bag shops are right on top of one another.'

'One carrier bag missing,' Iles replied. 'In a bush, according to your father, and then taken by the wind.'

'You haven't found that?' Jill said. 'God. Detectives? But even so – and even if she went to the pictures or theatre, she had hours over.'

'Some private interlude?' Hazel asked Iles. 'Our thinking.'

'This is your own mum you're talking about,' Darren said.

'Right,' Jill replied.

Iles brought the big plates of food over for Sarah and himself and they sat down and began to eat. Iles said through fried bread: 'Scott, I've spent my life coping with people loath to be associated with me. The Chief. Harpur. Ministers of religion, naturally. A brother and sisters. Your parents are in a grand tradition. You must never think badly of them.'

'I do,' Scott said. 'It's yellow.'

'They're not paid not to be yellow,' Iles replied. 'And now and then or oftener some of us who *are* paid not to be yellow are very yellow – myself, the Chief, especially the Chief, Harpur, though never Erogenous Jones.'

'OK, I'll try to come at Christmas,' Scott said.

'I've got a suit in the car which will about do you for the funeral,' Iles replied. 'I'm always equipped for a flit, like W. C. Fields. Dark tie – a London club job.'

'If there's danger – reprisals and so on – shouldn't the children take special care now, Colin?' Daphne asked. 'Hazel out of the house all day yesterday, unaccounted for. Besides which, technically they're both still under age.'

'Oh, I expect she was close by with good and well-trusted friends, Mrs Pointer,' Iles replied.

'Yes.' Harpur said.

'And it might, indeed, be more restful with us at Christmas,' Clifford said. 'Away from this difficult scene.'

'Mum's been given a really good, well, examination?' Hazel asked.

'The best,' Iles replied.

'As Jill says, we're thinking of DNA tracing,' Hazel told him. 'Identification of a contact through, say, semen.'

'Within the time limit?' Jill ground on.

'My God,' Daphne said.

'We just want to be sure Desmond Iles is up to date,' Hazel said. 'I mean, that uniform's the Crimean War.'

'All that has been taken care of,' Iles replied.

'Such things as lovers' tiffs,' Jill said. 'Sometimes they can blow up into – Well, Darren and I, don't we, sometimes? Swearing and punching at least.'

'And thanks for the rail fare,' Hazel said.

'I don't understand?' Iles replied.

'Dad said it was him, claiming credit in his way, but we'd know differently,' Jill said.

'What's this about?' Clifford asked.

'I don't think I'd mind seeing Mum now,' Jill replied.

Scott put on Iles's magnificent double-breasted navy suit and knotted the Travellers' or whatever tie on his bare neck above a Green Party T-shirt. They went in three cars to the funeral home and assembled around Megan in a curtained, dark-carpeted side room with mahogany-type panelling and very reasonable muzak. 'They've done a good job,' Jill said, somehow keeping her voice steady. 'It's brought out all the best things in her face. You can see why men would go for her. Even now you can see it. The glossy shroud stuff sets her off.'

'I'm going to kiss her eventually,' Hazel replied. 'I definitely will.'

'So why couldn't you go for her, Dad?'

'I did.'

'But why not *only* for her?' Jill said.

'Jill, love, there's more than one way of looking at that,' Harpur replied. 'But you know, obviously.'

'I think, this sort of situation, people should just be quiet, watching with full respect and grief,' Scott whispered.

'The boy's right,' Clifford replied.

'Sometimes it simply isn't on for a husband, a wife, to think only of the other, Jill,' Sarah said.

'You *would* say that, wouldn't you?' Hazel replied.

'Yes, you would, wouldn't you?' Iles said.

'Christ, I don't have to defend myself to you, you of all people,' Sarah yelled at him across Megan.

'Please,' Daphne Pointer said. 'The noise will bring attendants. This is my daughter.'

'She was a very lovely, good woman,' Harpur said.

'I think so,' Iles replied.

'Why?' Hazel said.

'It was obvious,' Iles replied.

'But did you know her – I mean, really well?' Hazel asked. She, Harpur and the two Pointers bent in turn and kissed Megan.

'Not me,' Jill said. 'The cold would stay on my lips.' She gave a small, infinitely friendly and infinitely final wave, though, as they all left the room. 'Those tunes – she'd throw up.'

'They do their best, Jilly,' Daphne Pointer said.

'It's Jill,' Hazel replied.

Sarah drew a finger lightly across Harpur's wrist in the corridor. 'You're all right, Col?'

'All right.'

'I mean, really all right. Not alone?'

At the crematorium they had to wait in an ante-room for a time while another funeral was concluded. The Chief was in uniform, too, looking as unkempt as ever and sick. Perhaps Iles had it right and Lane was a kind and lovely man but no longer much of a cop. Iles usually did have things right. Harpur saw a good crowd of other police and police wives, and again felt grateful because Megan had always kept most of them at arm's length. Her Fortnightly friends were there in fair force, also, and in the chapel, one of them, a heavy, round-voiced woman, gave a decent address and a couple of the men read poems. Harpur sat in the front row between the two girls and Darren and Scott. Jill started to weep at

> Strew on her roses, roses
> And never a spray of yew.
> In quiet she reposes:
> Ah! would that I did too.

Harpur thought them good, smart lines, another game try by literature at proving the dead lucky. If you believed that, you could give up murder hunts. He drew Jill against him again and she stayed sobbing with her face into his scarf when the red curtain went over. Iles, sitting behind, tapped Harpur on the shoulder. 'Yes, he was here,' he whispered, 'looking bad.'

Jill came up, blotched. 'Who? Some paramour?'

'Well, he has his rights and feelings, I suppose,' Hazel said.

'That murky poem,' Jill replied.

'I know, I know,' Iles said. 'But a bit later there's the *vasty hall of death*. That gets the dignity back into things.'

Chapter 17

One of Megan's super-dreads was that one day they would be in the London flat when the owner or another set of guests arrived. God knew how many other keys were around. Tambo said it could never happen, but this did not comfort her, or not much. She found the thought of such precise timetabling odious: the confidential, hint-filled phone conversations that must go on – Tambo booking the place, and then the cleaners ordered to move in afterwards. She knew her attitude was stupid. If they wanted to be undisturbed, arrangements must be made. Adultery was rich in contradictions, though.

These angsts were her own special post-coital blues. They arrived on time today. Before they made love and while they made love her attention was commandeered. Afterwards, worries set in. Her head on a silk pillow case, her body between silk sheets, she would gaze about the bedroom – the first-division repro furniture and soothing William Morris style green wallpaper – feeling . . . not soothed. Who else came here? Was it watched? What was this flat – someone's showy *pied-à-terre*? If so, he, or she, must be worth plenty, to be able to keep such a place on stand by. And two more? One opposite?

Or perhaps the flats belonged to a company, available for its executives and valuable overseas customers. That might explain the characterless, impersonal feel here. There were pictures on the walls, but pale rural and fishing-boat jobs, picked for innocuousness. On their arrival the flat always smelled not so much clean as cleansed, as if all traces of the most recent occupants had been urgently removed. Would it have been better if she and Tambo were in the hotel they had used on earlier London meetings – a down-market hotel, the sheets non-silk, even non-fresh? At least that place was theirs for the time they bought. Here, they were, yes, grace and favour occupants, and she learned a long time back that where police were concerned favours had to go two ways, and grace meant tit-for-tat services.

'Shall we eat here?' Tambo asked after they had dressed. 'There are meals in the freezer.'

'Of course there are. No, please, let's go out somewhere.' Another contradiction: after all, she guzzled the champagne and used the bed. Why quibble over cartoned seafood platter? She wanted to be away from here, that was all.

'Fine,' he said.

Her anxieties in 26A were not about danger. Nobody was going to let himself in to do them harm. Why should anyone, no matter who it belonged to? The watcher and the VW had pushed her askew? If there *was* a watcher. But she would be ashamed if discovered in the flat: especially ashamed to be discovered in bed, and not keen to be found making tea or watching television. Domesticity would look false and, or, sleazy to anyone in the know, and anyone who came here would be in the know. Deeper than that, though, she would hate to confront the truth about this place. The thought of sitting in on a conversation between Tambo and the owner appalled her. Naturally, that would be kept vague and harmless if she were listening. She was used to catching bits of such coded chats between Colin and his special contacts, as he called them. And she was used to getting hold of the words and squeezing from them fragments of what was actually being said behind those references to 'business', to 'opportunities,' to 'substantial gratitude'. Christ, this crafty quid pro quo-ing was one of the things that poisoned her marriage, and ultimately made her feel humiliated by contact with Colin and dependence on him. Now, it had followed her here?

'Will you be thought ungrateful?' she asked.

'Ungrateful?'

'Not availing ourselves of the freezer grub. We could pre-tend we've eaten the meals – drop them in a street litter bin, out of this district.'

'They're not compulsory, Megan.'

She had hurt him, and was almost sorry. At home, she used to give the same sort of pain to Colin sometimes by stridently querying his off-white deals. She felt entitled. She felt duty bound. No longer could she manage that with Colin, though, because he now ignored the attacks. He had come to think her unredeemably liberal-prim. He must have decided he could not run his job and kowtow to such qualms, so made his choice. And she made hers. Yes, she had better remember that. Turning from her arid survey of the opulent, dud room, she kissed Tambo on the neck and deftly straddled him. In so many of the sexy films she saw these days, the woman went on top. And then there was Germaine Greer, years ago, saying that any woman could be good underneath but real skill and commitment were needed when you rode. Commitment was so important. Greer had tempered her pronouncements with age, but Megan had years to go yet.

'I'm going to have you,' she said.

'I like the idea.'

'And we'll still have time to eat out. But no rushing this.'

'Right.'

In the restaurant she felt happy again, liberated, full of the future. There was a mirror behind Tambo and in it she thought she appeared splendidly at ease – her eyes a bit beyond bright and almost flashy, her skin good, her hair natural. The beginnings of a grown-up but uncynical smile were built permanently into her lips and ready to get bigger, and she felt that if she saw a face like that on another woman she would assume fine times ahead for her, as long as she had boldness and certainty. She had. She was thirty-six, considered that she looked it and that she looked content to look it. And now and then she did.

She might be all wrong about the flat. At this table in this cheerful and bustling eatery she did not need to find out one way or the other, and she could talk to Tambo in her own vague and harmless style of their relationship.

Tambo said: 'Sorry if I seemed to be forcing the pace. Wanting us to be properly together.'

'It's flattering.'

'I get impatient. I get worried. Time might pull you deeper and deeper into home life, marriage.'

'I don't think so.' She was not as naïve as Colin believed, and did see that moral absolutes might not always be available to police, any more than to statesmen or popes or wives. This failed to make Colin's endless grey-area work tolerable to her, though. She did not want to live alongside his nod-and-wink arrangements, the secret pacts. And this pushed her into what she recognized as craziness: she decided she must forget the possibility 26A most probably came to Tambo when it did by such a nod-and-wink, secret agreement.

Oh, but this restaurant was her sort of milieu – not an especially expensive place, near Shepherd Market, and not in the same league as the borrowed flat, but pleasantly busy, relaxed, with a babble of talk in a mixture of languages, good Italian food and unservile waiters. 'Darling, I do keep all those things in mind, all the time,' she told Tambo. 'The long-term future.'

'I get selfish, that's the truth of it.'

'I like that.'

Her parents would not look happily on the change she was thinking about. Hard luck. They were not always right, though often. She wished she knew why Hazel and Jill disliked them. The girls saw through people pretty well, and it would be good to have their analysis: might help Megan discount her parents' views. The Pointers' coolness towards police could not explain it: the girls would endorse that and throw in outright enmity to police as a breed, though not necessarily to Colin as father. Jill once muttered 'phoney' when Megan asked her why she and Hazel could not get on with the Pointers. She wouldn't elaborate though, or couldn't.

Chapter 18

And then, at the bread-and-butter pudding stage, Megan felt this restaurant was a waste of time. During the spaghetti she had glanced up again at the mirror and decided that, among all those other qualities, she looked tonight exceptionally bedworthy, even for her and even though she'd already been repeatedly bedworthy for most of the afternoon. It was something to do with her lips and mouth, glossy from vongole. Naturally, it was: everyone knew why mouth and lips did that although lateral. So why wasn't she still in bed? Tambo was right, and they should have stayed at the flat. They were here only as a tribute to her nerviness. Well, stuff that. Could she go on for ever being sniffy about the job morals of her men? Too much damage had already been done between her and Colin, and it was insane to open the same holy war against Tambo.

The guilt that struck earlier, when Tambo called her a home-maker, returned now, and she began to eat quickly, wanting to be out of this place and to reaffirm things with him where these things were best reaffirmed. They could probably get another hour at the flat before her train. He noticed the acceleration and read what it meant, then began to rush his dessert, too. They both grinned. For God's sake, who ever heard of an Italian restaurant serving bread-and-butter pudding, anyway? The rage in Rome?

'Skip the coffee etcetera?' Tambo asked.

'Well, *their* etcetera.' On the train afterwards she realized this was probably the moment when her resolve to leave Colin took real shape. Tambo had earned commitment.

He paid and they left. Outside, she thought she might have

heard from somewhere fairly close that Germanic, pushy, small-scale roar of a Beetle. She looked about, but saw no yellow vehicle. In any case, this was early evening Mayfair – Piccadilly one side, Park Lane the other – so you expected traffic din, especially near Christmas: maybe a Beetle in it, maybe not, and, if so, maybe a yellow one, maybe not. Someone tailing would use a noisy, bright yellow car? Was she growing obsessive about VWs? She could not let niggly fearfulness return and spoil the time left. You had to give passion a run.

Nobody had moved in at the flat. Joke. Of course not: Tambo must have a full night's reservation.

'Yes,' he said, when they were leaving again, 'perhaps I will ditch those meals somewhere. Foolish to give offence.' He brought them out and removed the boxes. He levered the frozen food intact from the cartons with a knife and then placed all containers and foil in the waste bin. Each actual dinner slab he put in a side pocket of his jacket.

Megan said: 'After the oven, the cartons would be messy. And then what about dirty plates and cutlery?'

'We could have washed up and replaced them.'

'We never wash anything.'

'It's only cleaners we have to fool.'

'They report back to someone? Big Mr Big, with three Careen Street places? That scares you?'

'Look, let's not make a meal of this, Megan. Frozen.'

He was right. Hadn't she planned to be tolerant? When they kissed goodbye at the station she put a hand against his jacket and could feel one meal like a hardback pocket Bible. She was about to offer to bin both for him on the train but then thought, Sod it. Do your own sucking up, Tambo. Better still, he might forget and finish with pockets full of halibut bits and prawns in Niçoise sauce. Then she changed her mind again. She mustn't be vindictive. Tambo was her future. 'Give me the rations. I'll throw them away.' She pushed both into a side pocket of her handbag.

Chapter 19

Back at the house after the cremation, Erogenous Jones broke away from the Chief's group and approached Harpur, holding an untouched glass of discount red, features very confidential, even for Erogenous. 'Know anyone in a black or navy Panda, sir?' he asked. 'One lurking at the funeral, then possibly behind you and yours most discreetly on the way back here? Girl, twentyish. People use all sorts to keep an eye these days. But it could be absolutely nothing at all.'

Or something. Sergeant Jeremy Stanislaus Jones – Erogenous by repeated testimonials – was a supreme tail, and so a supreme counter-tail. All he needed was a bit of self-discipline to go with it and they might yet make him inspector, just in time for retirement and a better pension.

'Here's a number, sir.' Erogenous stuck out one finger of his free hand and Harpur glanced at a ballpoint registration.

'A mystery,' he said.

'Really?'

Mystery meant virgin in street lingo. Definitely not that. 'A puzzle,' Harpur said.

'I've mentioned nothing elsewhere, Col, in case it's imagination. Probably. This would be a nice-looking kid, judging from a distance. Oh, possibly a reporter. The funeral's news.'

'Yes.'

He stuck the finger out again. 'I haven't asked the computer for an owner.'

'I see.'

'I thought you might wish to deal with it.'

'Yes.'

'But if you want me to take a—'

'No, perhaps I'll have a stroll outside in a minute anyway. Who knows? And some air.'

'Understandable.'

Erogenous edged away. Harpur had said the girls could produce the whisky and gin after a couple of hours and Jones put his untouched plonk on the Critical Theory bookshelf and took a couple of heavy Bell's, one in each hand, from Hazel. Then he rejoined Lane's party with the Pointers.

Harpur was delighted to see the good mixture of people who had returned to the house. Megan probably would not have worried either way: esteem from others she could take or leave alone, she was so cocky. Megan did enjoy a good party, though, and good meant mainly very few police, or none. Today, there were bound to be some. Protocol as well as genuine sympathy required Lane and his wife to show, and so others would follow. But police were outnumbered. As for Harpur, he valued public regard and thought Megan deserved plenty. Police needed it, too, but were getting less and less. He longed to believe but couldn't that if it were *his* funeral there would also be a big and various crowd, not just relatives, the job, and prosecution lawyers. Ah, well, you joined for free notebooks and the pension, not a consensus cortège.

Jill approached with two people Harpur thought he recognized. 'Here's Coral and Roger from Mum's Fortnightly, Dad. They've been looking for you. Something important to say, apparently.'

'Most kind of you to come,' Harpur replied. He would place them in a minute: Coral, fairish, small, birdy nose, clever eyes, and Roger, plump and plump faced, a teacher's mouth, not too bright looking, but a stayer.

Earlier, with Darren's help, Harpur had pushed the Christmas tree into a corner, decorative lights off. Megan, Hazel and Jill had heavily paperchained all the downstairs, and Harpur decided it was too much labour to remove for mourning. As Iles had said, best recognize Christmas would survive regardless. Besides Coral and Roger, several other regulars at Megan's Fortnightly had come on to Arthur Street, plus official Education contacts and members of the parent-teachers' association at John Locke Comprehensive, their daughters' school. Megan had been a governor there. It pleased Harpur that the girls would see how generally prized their mother was. Although his daughters acted terse and blasé, they remained children, with children's weaknesses and needs.

'On the train with Megan,' Roger said, 'Obviously, we've already talked to some of your colleagues yesterday,' Roger said. 'An Iles? Garland?'

'They're here now,' Harpur replied.

'Long-time friends of Megan, you see, and proud to have been so,' Roger said.

'Of course,' Harpur replied. 'I recognized you at once.'

Coral glanced at Jill. 'We didn't exactly tell Mr Iles and Mr Garland everything. It seemed wise to speak to you first. I mean, in view of the sensitive nature. We owed it to Megan.'

Jill said: 'You want me to clear off?'

'This was by no means withholding evidence,' Roger said. 'Just timing. You would be free to pass everything on, naturally, Mr Harpur.'

'You want me to clear off?' Jill said.

'This is in a way speculative, we'll admit that,' Roger replied.

'Questioned by Mr Iles – well, something daunting about him?' Coral said. 'Yet a kind of politeness. One drew back from full disclosure. Somehow.'

'People are like that with Des Iles,' Jill replied. 'Coral, did he make any, you know, well, approach – admiring your body and so on? But behind it all, he has good intentions. Often. Dad says.' She walked across the room and took another Bell's to Erogenous.

'This had been an extremely pleasant coincidence, bumping into Megan on the train,' Roger said, 'someone for a good chat and so on, and even reading her a facetious little poem of mine, about which she was so appreciative. I was delighted by this and preoccupied, but Coral thinks—'

'I wondered if she was travelling with a man, you see, Mr Harpur. Forgive my saying so. I mean, clandestinely. In fact, I grew certain she was.' Coral looked appallingly sad and anxious. She was whispering and occasionally her voice fell so far Harpur could hardly hear.

'Yes,' Roger said, 'perhaps Coral should speak of this her-self. Certainly. Might I give you a copy of the poem, Mr Harpur? It's flippant, yes, but might have some value to you, since she heard it only minutes before . . . before that terrible matter.'

Harpur took the paper and put it in his pocket. 'Thank you, Roger. I'll read this later and place it with mementoes of her.'

'The only other odd thing is just before we arrived Megan went to the toilet, taking her handbag, naturally,' Roger replied. 'Well, make-up and so on, I expect. And then, on the seat where the bag had been, what turned out to be a piece of fish, as it appeared. No, definitely. I've checked subsequently. This was a small piece of what could be turbot or halibut, maybe, in what looked like a sauce, and part frozen, just thawing. I recovered it.'

From his pocket he brought a small, transparent plastic bag with the piece of fish in it, still mostly white but the edges greening. He handed it to Harpur. 'Please, do keep it. Of significance? I don't know.'

Harpur put this into his pocket, also. 'Thank you, Roger.'

'As if shaken from an outer compartment of her handbag when she moved it, going to the toilet,' Roger said. 'This was an oddity, in my view. I would have jokingly asked her about it, but she remained in the toilet even after the train had drawn in and we disembarked and didn't talk again. How anyone could be carrying fish pieces in a handbag, I mean.'

'What man was this, Coral?' Harpur asked.

'In an expensive dark overcoat, possibly camel hair.'

'Fur collar,' Roger said.

'Youngish. Say twenty-four, five, dark moustache. As we joined Megan, I saw him approaching from the next carriage or the one before. As if, say, he had been searching for the buffet. His eyes were on Megan, it seemed to me, very much so. My impression – as Roger says, speculation, yet almost a certainty – was he was returning to resume sitting with her. Then, when he saw us with Megan, he seemed to change direction, pretended – that's speculation again, of course – but pretended he was making for the lavatory. Which he did, and then must have gone to some other part of the train, to join up later. Tact? We couldn't see because we were on inside seats with Megan by then. She probably could. He certainly didn't pass where we were, though.'

'What I've also wondered since then, re the fish,' Roger said, 'was if they'd had a meal from the buffet and it was poor, not cooked right, not thawed properly. He might have taken it back, but dropped that piece accidentally. Which would mean it had not come from Megan's handbag. That would be more credible.'

'Would it, though? I don't believe there is a buffet or restaurant car on that late train,' Coral said. 'I thought we asked once. I felt he had searched in vain, maybe looking for a sandwich for in the car. In any case, a buffet doesn't give out cooked meals to eat in the carriages.'

'You saw this man again?' Harpur asked.

'She definitely went to the same toilet, but we're pretty certain he was not still in there,' Roger replied.

'I don't know about that,' Coral said. 'All I could see was that the lighted sign at the end of the carriage came up FREE, but this operates if you only pull the bolt back. He could have waited in there. What I meant about sensitive, you see – in front of Jill. That is, meeting in a lavatory. If it was so.'

'In a way, I have to say this, she went towards the toilet quite urgently. I mean, yes, as if rendezvousing.'

'So did you see him at all again?' Harpur asked.

'On the station, waiting, I thought,' Coral said. 'Trying to keep out of sight, in shadows. To be frank, it looked like someone being discreet again. Leaving the train, both of them, but not being seen together? Especially by us. Do you know what I mean, Mr Harpur?'

'Again, sensitive,' Roger said.

Coral began to cry quietly. 'Look, I thought we were *de trop*.'

'One could always say there was something charmingly unconventional, even bohemian, about Megan,' Roger said. 'I don't mean just possibly carrying the fish, which could be of no importance at all, but her general lovely way. To do with the arts, and we felt her life was her own and we shouldn't pry or interfere. She was entitled to travel with whomsoever she wished in any direction and at no matter what hour. I believe she might have regarded Coral and me as rather staid and bourgeois, despite what is actually quite a frank poem, as you'll see, and, teaching college literature, I could be deemed on the bohemian fringe myself, I suppose.'

'And we simply left her to it,' Coral whispered, still weeping. 'Christ, we wrote her off, Mr Harpur.'

Jill must have seen her distress and came back. Taking Coral's hand she stroked her wrist gently. 'You really loved her, did you? Yes, she was grand. Loved her just as a friend, I mean, obviously.'

Iles also had spotted Coral crying and joined them with Sarah. 'We all understand the special pain you feel, Coral, Roger, being among the last to see her alive. But you must not blame yourselves. Colin would not want that.'

'There's no blame,' Harpur said.

'Not to have helped,' Coral muttered.

'How could you have helped, love?' Iles replied. 'You saw her on the train, talked to her, Roger read aloud his literature, you said goodbye. How could you have expected trouble? Please, please, don't persecute yourself.'

'Just the same,' Coral said. Sarah put an arm around her and she and Jill drew her away to a chair. Roger followed.

'That little cow's told you something she kept from me, Harpur?' Iles enquired.

'I don't know what she told you, sir.'

'What I've just outlined. There was something else?'

'Just as you've summarized it, sir.'

'And what did the Keats figure give you? Did I see some exchange?'

'Only a copy of the poem, sir.'

'I'll tell you what it looked like to me, shall I? Shall I, Harpur? A coke sachet. White powder? What goes on here? You're snorting? He runs stuff to you? What is this situation?'

'In his thoughtful way, sir, he decided the poem might serve as keepsake.'

'Shall I see it?'

Harpur brought the poem out and handed it to him.

Iles said: 'Of course, I've seen it already. I fart at thee.'

'From the poem? They're blunt, some of these writers.'

'Don't fucking brick-wall me, Harpur. Your usual damn secrecy games? This is a house of grief. Try to remember a woman who was quite close to you is dead, and show respect. I could feel Coral closing down when I interviewed her, editing stuff out, one of those statements more hole than matter, *il y a des lacunes* – for me, but maybe not for you. Listen Col, how the hell did she come to be linked to a piece of grease like Rog? Considerable, experienced legs. Ever tried anything there? I don't object to a Stanley knife nose. Then again, could one go anywhere Roger's going? Does he, though – so busy with the poetry? So, they had some little insights, information for your ears only?'

Harpur went to talk to Avril Cater, who had done the crematorium address. He especially wanted her and the verse readers to hear of his and the girls' gratitude. And, as far as he was concerned, anyway, Harpur certainly meant it. He felt almost sure this was the sort of service Megan would have fancied, though he could be wrong. Occasionally, in Megan's life and now, today, it struck him as tragic that he could never really tell how she might react on major choices. Once, he had mentioned this to Iles who said such blind and blundering intimacies ensured marriage was what it was, doomed.

'You really captured her in your talk, Avril,' Harpur said.

'Those trips to town were for Megan, ironically, a lifeline – to be in touch for a little while with theatre, off-main-street cinema, galleries, she found crucial. All the more foul she should be killed like that, after such a restorative time. She was in all the best senses cultured and helped others to enjoy and find nourishment in culture. Well, I've seen even you in some of the Fortnightly sessions here, haven't I?'

'Oh, yes,' Harpur replied, 'whenever I had—'

She interrupted him with a big, coarse, chesty laugh and lightly punched his lapel three times, slowly, then fingered the wool mixture cloth in vamp style, like foreplay. Christ, she could not be making a but-life-goes-on proposition, here, now, could she? 'All right,' Avril said, 'you came out of politeness – thought it all rubbish.'

Harpur said: 'Not at all. I—'

Hazel approached with a part-used bottle of Aussie Chardonnay in one hand. She was still in her funeral gear – jeans, wicked-governess black boots and one of Harpur's old red and silver check shirts. She refilled Avril's and Harpur's glasses. In the other hand, Hazel carried a can of Vimto for herself. 'That service today, utterly heathen,' she said.

'Secular it's called, Hazel. We thought this was what Megan would want.'

'Sure of it,' Avril stated.

'Avril, my mother's gone wherever endorsed with a scrap of was it Arnold and some lines of an Edna St Vincent Millay, I gather, plus your thoroughly nice thoughts. If you ask me, she needed a major absolution sluicing, top to toe, front and back, yet not a dog collar in sight.'

'I'll take responsibility for that,' Harpur said.

'Yes, but you're still alive and enjoying yourself,' Hazel replied. She took a long, meditative pull at her Vimto. 'What I've got, Avril, or had, is a couple of parents who couldn't care a monkey's about all the usual solid marriage things like loyalty, but who stayed together, slept together – etcetera, presumably – went to cocktail parties and might have had Christmas dinner together off Irish linen, all as happy as could be, it seemed. So, any wonder if, as one of their kids, I'm knocked sideways, don't know for sure what's what, start wondering what is there that's solid and real? Maybe it's religion. So, God's a myth. A decent myth might be an advance – more substantial than anything around here. For instance, when she went on these London trips did she ever ask one of you lot to go with her, the objectives being so alleged arty? *But you must come, Avril, Maurice, Geraldine. We'll have such a rave at* Titus Andronicus *in the park, or* JFK.'

Avril said: 'I would trust Megan to—'

'Go after whatever she wanted. Solo. So would I,' Hazel replied. 'And I'd trust Dad to do the same. Both ungovernable, unprincipled, unrumbled. Where does that leave me? How do we deal with them at school when they say my mother got what she asked for, shagging around by Inter City?' Her voice went high and Scott sidled up and put a hand on her head for a second.

'I don't believe they do say that,' Harpur answered.

She shrugged and had another thoughtful, noisy pull at the can. 'What they're thinking, especially staff.'

'Some staff are here, love, very cut up,' Harpur said.

'Your words in the crem, Avril – as I say, decent. Yet missing the complexities? My mother was great but not eulogizable. Yes, Jill's word about your effort, bland.'

'I'm sorry,' Avril said.

'We could have taken the truth,' Hazel replied. 'Some of it's unpainful.'

'You're a bit severe, Hazel,' Harpur said. He moved off as if to circulate and left the house and walked along Arthur Street. It was cold without a coat, but he wanted the amble to look unplanned. At the top, he turned into Edward Street, then another turn into Albert Gardens and was on his way slowly back to the house when a black Panda pulled in just ahead of him and stopped. He opened the passenger door and climbed in. Denise said: 'Oh, Colin, is this unforgivable? Her funeral. The baked meats. These streets – a tour of Queen Victoria's family. I'm going back tonight, but I had to see you.'

'Denise, love, whose name is the car in?'

'Daddy's.'

'Good.'

'I've been spotted? So, who'd fall for a cop? Why do you have to worry now? You're a widower. I thought I saw one of your children going into the house after the fire, nestling against you, maybe crying.'

'Jill.'

'That's terrible for you.'

'They're both being pretty good. Strong.'

'Look, you needn't kiss me. I suppose it would seem gross. Today. I definitely understand.'

He kissed her, holding her face between his hands and not hurrying.

'I saw about her on TV and in the papers,' Denise said. 'Poor Colin.'

'Poor Megan.'

'Using her to hurt you? Like they tried to with me? You've got too many women. Hostages to what-you-call. And then I couldn't phone. Your house would be full – police, relatives, I knew it. Bloody university vacation, so I'm all those miles away from you. I stayed home in Stafford and watched it in every bulletin and read about it in three tabloids and told myself to stay out of it because I was not part of it, just a student you liked and screwed twice a week in term but not really, well, yes, not really *part of it*. Then today I couldn't take it any more and just drove. I said stocking up with library books before the Christmas shut-down.'

'Well, I'm glad you came.'

'Honestly?'

'Of course.'

'Even today, Col?' She was looking away from him, out of the driver's side window when she said the next bit, speaking very deliberately. 'They think they can hurt you worse by killing her than killing me? Why did the sods decide that? What's their bloody evidence for that? Tell me. Did you need me, Col? I mean, at a time of shock and so on did you find you really needed me? Only me. This would be important.'

'Of course.'

'Don't keep saying of course. Jesus, I'm up against a marriage here. Death underlines things. And the sorrow of children. Honestly, I told them at home I'd be back tonight, so you don't have to take me to a hotel, anything like that. Even if you wanted to you definitely couldn't.'

'There's a sort of party in the house. I ought to be about.'

'I saw the cars and your curtains aren't drawn. That's what I mean – what I'm up against. A social context. I'm the face at the window. Christmas trimmings. And then there's those flowers at the place. On television. I bet you've been up there. But that's all right. You'd have to, I see that, honestly, police-wise and husband-wise. How often? She must have been liked.'

'She knew all sorts.'

'This was a deep thing between you, regardless. What a stupid remark. Of course it was – two children, all those years.'

'I ought to go back, Denise.'

'Plus her parents there, I suppose. Yours dead, but they would have come, too.'

77

'Maybe.'

'What I'm up against. A death like that can bring a marriage alive, the whole dynasty assembles.'

'They did what they wanted, my parents. They never got on with Megan, so who knows if they'd have bothered?'

'So why didn't they get on with her?'

'They didn't get on with anybody. My father lost patience with people when he was tight, and he often was.'

'But there was something special about her they couldn't get on with? A hateful aspect?'

'No, I don't think so. Megan was never hateful.'

'Always you have to defend her, don't you?'

He kissed her again, briefly this time and opened the door. Erogenous was right, she did look lovely, even after the winter motorway and jealousy. This was a wonderful girl, and unbelievably caring, for somebody so young. 'Go carefully and don't forget the books.'

'Oh, fuck off, family man. I could have rung them and said I was staying over – bad weather.'

She drove briskly past him near the house, but did not seem to look, eyes staring ahead, her face rigid and proud, giving him the big ignoral. When Harpur returned, Erogenous, watching from the window, asked: 'Any sign of that sticky Panda then, Col?'

'No.'

'I thought not. I'm getting old, you know, seeing spooks. But at least spooks with nice tits.'

Coral and Roger were talking to the Pointers, who looked sad but comforted. Harpur thought Megan's parents had been impressed with the crematorium service, to their surprise. He wanted to satisfy them – felt a duty to compensate for being who and what he was, and for what he might have brought on their daughter.

Leaving, the Chief and Mrs Lane came to say goodbye, Iles and Sarah with them. 'You bear up remarkably well, Colin,' Lane told him.

'Harpur's all control, sir, all sense,' Iles replied. 'And he knows he has such support. Yourself, Mrs Lane, friends. One talented friend has given him a poem for solace.' He handed it back to Harpur.

'That's remarkably touching,' Sally Lane said. 'An elegy?'

'Exactly,' Iles replied.

'This might be something for the Force newsletter,' Lane said. 'But perhaps you'd see it as too personal, Colin.'

'Exactly,' Iles replied.

The police contingent left soon after Lane, and then the Pointers went. Only Hazel and Jill and their boyfriends remained, and they started to clear up. Harpur helped for a while and then took another walk around the neighbouring streets, wearing a top coat now. This time, he failed to find the Panda, though. Denise could be impulsive and harsh as well as caring. Perhaps it was a good thing she had gone. As she had said, a certain level of behaviour was necessary today.

Chapter 20

At the station car park, fumbling for the Astra keys in her handbag, Megan found herself facing a tricky debate. She had set her carrier bags down on the snowy ground while this customary search took place. That would be all right: the snow lay thin and the night was cold enough to keep it dry, so in this brief pause dampness would not get through to mark the tablecloth or the tie for Colin or her fun-thing trousers. Christ, 'fun-thing' – the phrase must be two decades out of date. She'd have to watch that in London. Here, she might seem racy. There she could look and sound quaint. The tie, especially, she wanted perfect. It had developed into a farewell job – something to offset the yelling and screaming that were sure to come. She could not see much: overhead lights at the car park were routinely airgunned and a border of high trees deepened the darkness. When she lifted the handbag to nearer her eyes there was a whiff of fish and Megan winced. Rehearsing her quit statements on the train, she had forgotten for well over an hour to drop the frozen meals into a carriage refuse bin, and the food must have started to thaw. Perhaps there were one or two fragments still left in her bag. She would take a proper look in the light when she reached home: no glamour points in accessories stinking of fish.

What she debated was whether she should tell Colin tonight that she meant to leave, or wait for morning. Wouldn't it be farcically callous to climb into bed and sleep alongside him as normal, the announcement on hold? *Did you have a good night, Col? Oh, I'm buggering off for keeps at the end of the week.* Now and then, in his sleep or not in his sleep, he would put an arm around her when she came back late. It was the

80

habit of years, and had been a lovely, togetherness habit once: not particularly sexual but comradely. Besides, if she failed to speak at once would she chicken?

For a second or two she was caught in a departing car's headlights and someone gave a brief blast on the horn. That must be Coral and Roger, and she paused in her key search and turned to offer a good smile and a wave. She could make out Coral's profile against the passenger window easily enough but, although she did give a small wave back, Coral hardly turned to look towards the Astra. She seemed to have decided Megan wanted nothing to do with them and would resent being stared at. Mad. What was there for them to see, other than a woman mildly panicking again over car keys? But perhaps they realized she had deliberately escaped from them on the train, and were hurt and uptight. At the next Fortnightly she must make a fuss of both, even get Roger to present his indigestible poem.

And then she realized there would be no more Fortnightlies. She also realized that any piffling offence those two felt would be forgotten in the shock when they heard she had walked out and Literature at 126 Arthur Street had shut. Somehow, that rocked her – to visualize Coral and Roger getting the gossip. *God, though, these hot-arsed police wives*. She stood slightly dazed, momentarily not concerned to find the keys, and gazing after their car as if this separation were the first evidence of that bigger, agonizing separation now due. Watching the tail-lights disappear, she suffered a sudden, sharp loneliness in this hostile black slab of no man's land. Yes: at home in her childhood there had been a Great War picture book showing troops on patrol at night and suddenly lit up and targeted under a brilliant hanging star shell. Caught by the headlights, she had briefly felt exposed like those soldiers. All the other cars and passengers had gone. It was as if friends had written her off, aware of what was about to happen when she reached home.

This was mad, too. How could they know? Hadn't she only just decided? And, anyway, those two had never been friends: not people she would seek out, except at the Fortnightly. Feeble: she was slipping into self-pity when she ought to be joyful, resolute, greedy for the future, strong with hope and the prospect of change. Stuff Coral and Roger. This was not the Western Front but a city centre car park. Oddly, Colin had mentioned seeing that same star-shell picture in one of the few books at his parents' house, and talked of being suddenly pin-pointed in a similar dangerous way while on a police operation one night. They had strange links. But don't think of that now.

Where were the fucking keys? Triumphing, she cornered them in her bag, opened the boot and bent to pick up her London buys. Crouched over the carriers she took another decision and settled with herself that she should tell Colin tonight. It might be necessary to wake him. He always said people were at their lowest in the early hours – why police did house raids then. Give him a taste. Before putting her purchases into the boot, she methodically brushed the snow from the base of the bags, while her mind worked out a timetable. First, inform him right away, and possibly have a discussion. He might not want that immediately. Colin was entirely capable of grunting 'Right' at her declaration and sliding back into sleep. The shouting would come later.

Obviously, he and she should settle how it would be explained to the girls: Hazel and Jill must be told by her and Colin together soon, say at breakfast, and without theatricals. Colin would not put on a show in front of the girls. Afterwards, and while all of them were still present, she would give the pre-Christmas gifts, including Colin's tie, so the children could see it was not all bitterness. Probably nobody would be totally surprised, especially not the girls. They had the kind of intuition and antennae that were sure to piss off their men partners later. She might wear the new trousers. It was vital that the family part of the occasion should be chiefly positive, though obviously also sad.

Chapter 21

When Harpur returned from looking for Denise in her Panda, he found the Christmas tree had been brought back to the centre of the sitting-room and its lights switched on. This would be Hazel: she liked all that sort of thing now and then – optimism, myth, corn. It was nice in her. She was the sort of kid who might have held a marriage together, if there had been the least chance. Hazel was just old enough to want to hang on to bits of childhood occasionally. Jill was young enough to want to escape it. The girls had done some tidying and were in the sitting-room with Scott and Darren, these two and Hazel drinking cider, Jill on Vimto. Harpur got rid of the fish and Roger's poem in the kitchen waste, found himself just about enough cider and gin to make a helpful mix, and joined the four.

'We were discussing her ashes,' Jill said.

'They're collectable from today,' Harpur replied. 'But one option is the Garden of Remembrance at the crematorium. It's quite nice out there.'

'Mixed with all the others underfoot,' Jill said. 'Is that on, Dad?'

Someone rang the front door bell and Jill went to answer. Anxious suddenly, Harpur stood. It was late, and he felt on edge, worried for the girls. But did menace come to the front door? Jill returned with an angry, presentable woman Harpur did not recognize.

'Whose suit is that?' she screamed at Scott. 'Is this my boy? And tie? You're wearing *his* clothes. But, my God, you want to be mistaken for him?'

'Mr Harpur's twice as big as me, Mother, and fair. I'm not,' Scott replied. 'Not his suit at all.'

'Whose?'

'A friend's,' Harpur replied.

'So, police. Police only have police friends. They're using you, Scott, don't you see? That's police. I don't want you here, or even near here. In their clothes you're a target, like them. You know I've warned you, Scott, dear Scott. He knows this, Mr Harpur. This is criminal.'

'We were glad to see him today, Mrs Grant,' Harpur replied. 'Both lads. My wife would have appreciated it, believe me.' She would not take a drink, luckily, but Harpur gave her his chair and took the one at Megan's desk for himself. This seemed an invasion of her dull patch and he felt uncomfortable.

'Sitting here, curtains wide,' Mrs Grant said. 'And sending a young girl to the door at night. No security peep-hole. Where's safety? If you can't guard your own how can you guard the populace, Harpur? A wife out alone at that hour. I know there's grief here, and I'm truly, truly sorry, but I don't want Scott to go on seeing her, that's the upshot. It's at an end. This is a dangerous and vicious city, like all the rest, and you people can't cope.'

'Sometimes we have a victory, Mrs Grant,' he replied.

'Marginal.'

'Yes, perhaps.'

'We have to look after ourselves, and look after those close to us. To be blunt, you have failed us, are failing us, Mr Harpur. And the result of that has been borne home to you personally in this tragedy now.'

The Chief said pretty much the same from time to time. Perhaps they were right. Iles might have known how to answer her. Iles still thought a win possible, as long as you fought rough enough and perfected ways to beat the courts. Jill said: 'How can you have piled up so many fears in the time, Mrs Grant? You don't look *that* old.'

'This would be such a blow to Hazel, to lose Scott,' Harpur said. 'My girls are entitled to a life, regardless.'

'You're a target. Yours are a target,' Mrs Grant replied. She was tall, almost elegant, almost beautiful, a little hatchet-faced ultimately. She had the kind of body Iles, in fact, chased:

stately and energetic. The ACC felt cowed by big dignity in a woman, and was always stoked up by this reversal. 'Come now, Scott, we will speak our final respects about what might well have been a quite misunderstood lady and certainly no tramp and take our leave. We mean no reflection whatsoever, Mr Harpur, but in life there have to be certain divides, I fear.'

Hazel said: 'Mrs Grant, I'd expect someone like you to smell – a sewer smell? – but all I'm getting is *Rive Gauche*. Brilliant perfume.'

'Oh, stop that, Hazel,' Jill snarled. 'My sister's extreme, Mrs Grant. However, you *have* hurt her, us. But that's what you wanted?'

'Mrs Grant, I think there's room for more talk on this,' Harpur said. 'Scott has been a—' The telephone rang on the desk. 'Excuse me.'

It was Denise. 'I'm at The Tenbury, Col. I called home and said fatigue, and weather, and they advised by all means stay and lock the hotel room door. When can you get over? This is a flop-house, as you know. No night porter. Leave it too late and you won't get in, pardon the phrase.'

'It's so good of you to ring,' Harpur replied.

'People?'

'One or two.'

'Family?'

'*Inter alia.*'

'What I mean. The hard core still keening? Can you cut it, without seeming rude? If not, seem rude. Col, tell me something: am I safe? They go for Megan, they go for me – you and your job being the common factor? Or is this just me longing to sound as close to you as she was? I've heard of penis envy, but peril envy? But they did go for me once before. And your kids? Are they secure? People want to hurt you.'

'Thank you so much for your good words of sympathy. They are appreciated.'

'Col, am I safe?'

'We'll make it so.' He put the phone down. 'An aide to the Home Secretary,' Harpur told them. 'Kind to take the trouble.'

'I'll hang on here for a while, Mother,' Scott said.

Mrs Grant stood and stared down at him in his chair. She

85

had genuine grandeur about her now and the slightly hooked nose toned in. 'You're making a choice, you realize that?'

'I'll drive him home. If you wish,' Harpur said.

'No,' she replied. 'For God's sake no. Cars supposed to be anonymous but so old they draw attention. Not at my front door.'

'OK, a cab for him,' Hazel said.

'We'll put his head under a blanket from the door to the car,' Jill said. 'No identifying.'

'Well, remember, you've brought it on yourself, Scott,' Mrs Grant replied. 'None of this should be taken as reducing condolences, Mr Harpur. An entirely different issue and we sent a wreath.'

'Kind,' he said.

'Couldn't you draw the curtains?' she replied.

'Of course,' Jill said, and going to the windows pulled the cord. 'My mother thought it low-class to close them – i.e., not done by dukes in castles with grounds and the moat. I suppose we *are* low class now she's gone, and her parents. What class *are* police?'

The curtains did not come near to meeting in the middle and never had, and long ago Megan and Harpur decided to keep them open rather than spend on new.

When Mrs Grant had left, Hazel said: 'Going back to the ashes, Darren thinks they should be scattered at some lovely, favourite spot in the country or alongside a river. All of us present.' She sounded half convinced.

'Phoney,' Jill replied. 'She didn't think anything of countryside or rivers, did she, Dad? A city person. Highgate. Smart shops. Tarmac. Oh, she did the Green bit in her way now and then because it's still modish, but no commitment. I've seen her get barmily excited about a crow, sure it was a buzzard.'

'I wouldn't mind having her here, in some prominent position,' Hazel said.

'No, I wouldn't either,' Harpur replied. 'I'd like it.'

'An urn? Why?' Jill said.

'A mark of continuing closeness and love,' Scott said.

'Yes,' Harpur replied.

'Plus, an ever-present reminder of mortality,' Scott said.

'Yes,' Harpur replied. 'Also, it's what crook families do,

and they often hit a deep-down rightness and decency.'

'Do we need a vote or can we say it's settled then?' Jill asked. 'I think so. Discuss later where exactly in the house.'

Harpur stood. He put a fiver near the glass of Erogenous's wine in the Critical Theory section, and unnoticed during the girls' clean-up. 'For the taxi.'

Hazel, carrying her cider, came and stood near him. 'And we can get rid of all these fat books, can't we, Dad? Make this room part of a household, not a culture statement.'

'Some can go,' Jill replied.

'Dad, you're going out? That call?'

'Perhaps you're drawn back yet again, Mr Harpur, to where it happened,' Darren said. 'But might this bring you yet more pain?'

'Don't worry if I'm late,' Harpur replied. 'Hazel, go home with Scott in the cab and come back in it.'

'So, a fiver enough, this time of night?' Hazel asked.

He put three ones with the note. 'You tip too big, Hazel. Vulgar.'

'Is she going to be safe alone in a taxi, two, three in the morning?' Darren asked.

'You suddenly the voice of Mrs Grant, then?' Jill asked.

'When you book it say "Detective Chief Superintendent Harpur's house", Hazel,' Harpur replied.

'That's wise?' Jill asked.

Harpur considered it. 'No, maybe not. Not at present. Say some big villain's name – Cameron Carbiddy. You'll be fine then.'

'Do you think my mother's got it right, then?' Scott asked.

'Touch and go.'

There was not much drink left and the off-licence would be closed. Harpur took Erogenous's glass of red carefully into the kitchen where he had noticed a bottle marked *Vin de Table Supérieur* about half full. He poured Erogenous's into that, plus about an inch of Scotch he spotted in another discarded bottle and some lager dregs. This brought the contents up almost to capacity and seemed to improve the colour. He felt cheered. Finding a cork, he took the bottle with him in his overcoat pocket.

As he drove to The Tenbury, he thought about that sighting

of Tambo by Iles at the crematorium. To appear there would have taken some nerve. It meant Tambo considered he had rights, a position. Funerals were not private, but attendance signified. Things between them must have been pretty serious. Tambo might be desolated. Well, for God's sake, of course they were serious. One day – maybe when Jill was a few years older – Megan meant to go to him, Harpur knew that. As to the sitting-room curtains, he had seen her thinking it would be ludicrous to lash out on replacements when everything might be thrown into upheaval soon. He agreed and knew she saw he did.

It seemed wrong that Tambo should have had to sneak in and out like that. When someone was dead a lot of difficulties resolved themselves. The girls would have liked to meet him: try to sort out what Megan found there that was missing in Harpur, and quite probably approve her new choice. They would have been fair to Tambo and genuinely curious, not cold or rude. Harpur himself had reasonably good memories of him in Iles's present job. Of course, Tambo was nothing like as dirty or clever or brutal or twisted or two-timing as Iles, and so nothing like as capable. But women did not necessarily prize men who devoted their whole glorious soul to the destruction of crookedness. Mrs Grant might fancy someone like that, though. All things considered, he should mention her to Iles, those august flanks.

There was only one glass in Denise's room at the hotel and they shared it. Somewhere in his education Harpur had learned you did not swig wine from the bottle. She said solemnly: 'Bringing you here – it's just nerves, Col. I have to be sure of ownership after all that. I mean, the funeral, the taking stock with your family, the regrets. So, look at me, tell me what you see.'

'How do you mean?'

'What you see.'

She was seated on the end of the bed and he had the only chair in the room, a blue basket-work thing in a shadowy corner, half covering a spot where the wallpaper had been badly stained by what he hoped was coffee. They had had this room several times before, but it did not grow on him. 'A girl, nineteen, beautiful, worried, a bit breakable looking, as ever, lovely skin, lovely nose, lovely body, though clothed.'

'No, no, not all that, not the standard stuff,' she hissed.

'You let me go to the end, though.'

'Naturally. What I mean is, what do you really *see*.'

'Well, I—'

'Some outsider? Some fly kid who can't know what you're going though and who can't and won't understand what the years together did for you and her? The binding. Some pushy girl with no real idea?' She began to shout, answering these self-made charges. 'Don't forget I drove all this way in winter to be with you. Is that so superficial, so childish?'

'I'll probably have a look around myself and try to get who did it to her,' he replied. 'There's some information.'

She stared at him for a while, working on this, her eyes big with effort. 'Yes, that's an answer, I suppose. You still feel bound to her, obligated.'

'Oh, people are very scared, Denise. A duty to clear it up. I'm scared myself.'

'You don't get scared. Won't others do the clearing up?' She poured and took a drink from the tooth-brush glass. 'This is horse piss.' She handed it to him.

He drank, rolling it in his mouth. 'Myself, I like it. It's honest. A freshness, yet maturity. Yes, others will look, too. Oh, very talented and devoted men and women. But you see, Denise, I have this stupid habit. We all have: don't tell anyone anything unless you have to.'

'Anyone? Colleagues?'

'Well, yes, them especially.'

'What else are mates for but to keep in the dark?'

'A professional thing.'

'So when you say you're going after her . . . after her—'

'Killer.'

'Yes. You mean it's just the job talking, a sort of tic? Not special to Megan, personal to her and you?'

'Exactly.'

She took the glass back and poured some more into it, then drank. 'You could be right about this,' she said. 'Yes, honest is the word. I've come round. Perhaps it needs the more experienced palate.' She drank again, copying the savouring routine.

Harpur said: 'I call what I've got information, but that's putting it strong. It's absolutely private to me, though. I live by such stuff.'

She drank some more and then passed the glass to him. 'Obviously, I don't believe one sodding word of what you just said about why you'll hunt him down, Col, but I've got to like it or lump it, haven't I? Same as the cesspit wine. At least you tried to make your reasons sound sane. That's considerate. But you feel you owe her something, her personally, not as a client.'

'Perhaps.'

She nodded. 'Right. But, anyway, undoubtedly, some men would not have come out to a girl the night of a murdered wife's cremation.'

'That I accept.'

'Some men would not want to or even be able to make love.'

'Right.'

She began to undress. 'If you'd prefer not to go to bed, Col, I'll understand. Believe this. We'll talk only. Or you could just lie by my side, warming, companionizing only, out of genuine respect for her. That, too, would be sickening.'

He looked around. 'It isn't that kind of room. This is a fuck room or nothing.'

'I'll drink to that, even this,' she said, naked, hale, but still breakable looking, and taking a good, noisy pull from the bottle.

Harpur said: 'I definitely was not tailed here and I'll have a good look around when I leave. But lock the door after me. This is basic. No special fret. Well, even your parents advised that.'

Chapter 22

Harpur returned home again at just before 5 a.m. and found all the lights still on, including the Christmas tree, and Hazel wearing pyjamas and her school raincoat playing Scrabble with Iles in the sitting-room. Iles was checking some word of Hazel's in the dictionary and rubbishing her. He spared Harpur only a brief wave.

'Here's my problem, Dad,' Hazel said, 'I don't care to think of this one knowing more about what my mum was doing in London than I know, so I gave him a call around 3 a.m. and said urgent, but not something discussable on an open line. He's got to tell me what he knows. Hasn't he? But hasn't he, Dad? He's behaved all right, if you're interested. Well, I told him I've been with my boyfriend all day and half the night, and in addition he's very respectful of the mourning. Despite what's said, it's my belief the Assistant Chief has decent strands.'

Iles put the dictionary aside: 'No such word. On Megan's activities, I can see Hazel's point of view, Col. But, obviously, it's not something I could talk about to her without consulting you first.'

'This is crazy, Dad. Insulting. What am I, some kid? Stuff has to be edited for me?'

'Hazel said you might not come home tonight, Harpur, but I thought probably yes, in view of the occasion.'

'Look, Dad, what I'm not having is some cop, cops, familiar with my mother's private life, having it on file and me kept out. Maybe you, too, Dad. But who knows if you care?'

She had one of her quiet, convulsive weeps, her head low over the Scrabble board. Iles put out a hand to touch her arm in consolation but she pushed it away hard and destroyed a couple of words, the counters running all ways on the floor. As ever, Harpur was confused by the abrupt swing from belligerence to childlike frailty. Christ, it was going to be a job bringing up these two solo.

Hazel sorted herself out a little. 'Mr Iles wants to tell me she never stopped thinking about us, and that's brilliantly nice of him, a true welfare gimmick. But I reckon three to five hours unaccounted for on that day and I've got an idea she was not thinking ceaselessly about Jill and me then. That I don't blame her for. I do blame Desmond Iles for sitting on secrets and having a dirty little smirk.' Now, she raised her head, leaned across the Scrabble and put a hand on his shoulder like someone's mother. He was wearing a costly, traditional pin-stripe navy suit, tailored to laugh at modes. 'Sorry, sorry, Mr Iles. I don't think you would have a dirty little smirk. That's not your style of dirtiness at all. Never little. But you can't keep all this sealed away. You know the man she was with? You talked to him? You know where they went and for how long? I think I'm entitled to know, too. No, I don't think I'm entitled, not usually. But if *you* know, then I'm entitled to know. What I said – urgent.'

'I see this,' Iles replied.

'Yes,' Harpur said.

'On the other hand, as to entitlement, I wouldn't think of asking where you've been tonight, Dad.'

Iles said: 'Oh, I should think some postponed surveillance or similar, now the funeral is over, Hazel. Our business has to roll on. Evil men do not rest, so we don't.'

Harpur watched her decide this was too gross to answer. 'There's no drink to offer him,' she replied.

'I've a little wine in the car,' Harpur said. Dawn was coming up, pale, cold and lovely. Megan would have done her Med performance: shivered and spoken of many genial dawns seen at Grasse or Seville when holidaying with her parents. He recovered the bottle from the rear seat. There was about a quarter remaining. Denise had not wanted it left in the room because the bouquet made her eyes water. He poured the ACC and himself a glass.

Harpur said: 'Well, yes, I think Hazel's made her case.'

'I'd say so,' Iles replied, drinking. 'Who's your vintner, Col? It goes like this then, Hazel: your mother went to London from time to time to meet a man you may remember, known universally as Tambo, a police officer who worked here previously, masquerading in my job, as it happens. Perhaps you are too young. On the last visit, he tells me they shopped, went to his place for a while, then to a restaurant. He saw her to the train. I can timetable it fairly exactly. This was a serious, established relationship. But I don't know whether that's a comfort or not.' It was not like Iles to sound tentative, but he did.

' "His place for a while," ' she whispered. 'What while? What place?' She lifted the front lower chunk of her raincoat and wiped her face. 'Is this unbearable for you, Dad? Sorry, but—'

'Some hours,' Iles replied.

'Great. So, where?'

'That's important?' Iles replied. 'Is this rather obsessive, Hazel?'

'I told you, I don't want you knowing more than me. It has to be documented.'

'He's divorced. He has a small flat on the border of Highbury and Islington. He tells me they went there.'

'As usual?' she asked.

'Yes.'

'What do you mean, he tells you?'

'He tells me. I haven't asked for checks. It didn't seem important. Where else would they go?'

'You're saying the important matter is they were leg-overing, and the site's irrelevant?'

'None of it seems related to your mother's death, Hazel, love,' Iles replied. 'That's what has to interest Francis Garland and me. Interviewing Tambo was a formality.'

'I suppose.'

Iles said: 'We've got traces of frozen fish in her handbag, Col. In her *handbag*. Is this intelligible to you? And what looks like two thawed-out fish meals in the litter bin of her carriage. Garland got to the terminus before the rail people did their valeting.'

'So, fish dinners are significant?' Hazel grunted.

'Probably not,' Iles replied.

Hazel said: 'And what does Tambo report? Was she going to ditch us?'

'He says definitely not.'

Hazel gave a momentary, triumphant smile. Then she said: 'And he was pleased about that? My mother's just a bit on the side – that serious, established relationship! Oh, poor Assistant Chief – you can't win, can you?'

Iles said: 'Tambo told me—'

'She never stopped talking about Jill and me except when her mouth was full.'

Iles almost winced. 'Told me you and Jill were paramount in all her planning.'

'Us, yes. What about him – Dad?'

'Col? He *is* a difficulty. I would never say he's negligible.'

'I think you could go back to bed now, don't you?' Harpur said.

She ignored that. 'Tell me about this other, then, Mr Iles,' she said. 'No, I don't remember him. What sort of man. What did she find there?'

'He was amiable enough,' Harpur said.

'You're amiable, Dad. You're pathetically amiable.'

'Tambo was designed by a cliché manufacturer to illustrate what "clean-cut" means,' Iles told her.

'Yes, she'd like that,' Hazel said. 'Forties film heroes on video. John Wayne.'

'So how the hell did she fetch up with Col, then?' Iles replied.

'Perhaps he used to be clean-cut. I'll get out some old pictures. Were you, Dad?'

'Half-cut,' Harpur replied.

Iles said: 'Tambo? A passable, safe mind. Intellectually arid. Entirely unoriginal. Hence the promotion. Possibly not trustworthy – I mean in more profound ways than myself and most of us. Vulnerable. Such a mistake, that. Totally sold on all the higher bullshit. I've actually heard him speak of Madonna as the supreme popular culture construct, and I only met him twice.'

'Yes, that would get to Mum, too.'

Harpur sensed movement on the stairs and in a while Jill appeared. She had pulled on an old green track suit. The collar of her night dress showed very off-white over the top. 'I heard voices,' she said. 'Private?'

'Of course not, Jill,' Iles replied.

'Did we get the boys home all right?' Harpur asked.

'Scott's going to bring the suit back later, Mr Iles,' Hazel said. 'He wanted to say Up Yours to his mother.'

'I think we're slowly winning Youth over,' Harpur replied.

'Get stuffed, Dad,' Hazel said. 'We were talking about this lover boy, Jill.'

'What's he like?' Jill asked. She went and sat on the floor near Harpur and leaned her head sleepily against his legs.

'Socially conscious,' Hazel said.

'That would be up Mum's street. And the Pointers'. Why didn't you ever try that, Dad? Couldn't you fake it?'

'He was truly distressed,' Iles said. 'He thought very highly of your mother.'

Jill said: 'Jerk. He's no right to be distressed. This was a private death in a public place. He's nowhere.'

Harpur felt her begin to shake against his legs, though she did not appear to be crying. Watching her, Iles seemed to grow confused and at a loss. Then he said: 'Look, it's almost breakfast time again. This fine vintage has quite quickened my palate. How about I pop home and get the Buck's Fizz stuff once more? I'll give Sarah a shake. She'll love to turn out.'

'And the baby?' Jill said. 'Please.'

'Fanny? Of course. Have to. There's no sitter there today.' He stood excitedly. 'This is going to be a ball.'

'Sixties language?' Jill said.

While he was away fetching the champagne and orange and the other party guests, Harpur went into the kitchen and tipped the waste bag on to the floor. He found Roger's poem and the fragment of fish in its sachet, and left the poem. The piece of discoloured fish did not say much to him but, sitting on the floor next to the refuse, he brought the fragment out of its container and gazed at it on his palm for a few moments, as if it were at least an accidental memento, and possibly a clue. Then he replaced it in the plastic envelope and put this into his pocket. He cleared up.

Shortly afterwards, Jill came into the kitchen to start cooking. 'Is there something frantic about Iles, Dad? All this festive eating and drinking.'

'For your morale.'

'Really? Does he think Hazel and I are feeble or something?'

Chapter 23

In the car park, Megan stood on the passenger side of the Astra while searching for her keys, the carrier bags down on the snow to free her hands. When she found the keys, she moved to the rear and after fiddling for the lock in the blackness opened the tailgate, then came back and began picking up her purchases. She took a bag in each hand and lifted the two into the car. This methodical procedure struck her as the actions of a family person, a provider: she had been out to garner and was now systematically bringing in the sheaves.

Then, bending to recover the second pair of carriers, she thought she glimpsed someone standing among the trees which edged and shrouded the car park. This figure was on the far side of the car, the driver's, about twenty yards from the Astra. She was facing the passenger side and looking through its two rear windows as she straightened. The view was nothing like perfect: from her to the Astra, then across the width of the cabin and afterwards the twenty yards of dark car park to the wind-rocked privet and conifer trees at the perimeter. It was an outline, a slight thickening of the shadows, motionless. That 'someone' was the best she could do. She would have been unable to say man or woman and remained uncertain she had seen anything at all. It was not just the distance and the grubbiness of the windows: her eyes were still adrift after the glare of Coral and Roger's headlights.

Fear made two distinct moves against her. First, it came from the simple shock of sensing someone there, watching. Christ, it was getting on for 2 a.m., and she was alone now, in a black bit of nowhere. This was a sudden, almost disabling sharpening of what she had already felt – that sudden, chilly solitariness of her life. Then came a different sort of terror, which had anger mixed in: anger with herself, and with her faculties, because she could not be sure what she saw. This was intelligent dread based on the worry that her sight or her brain could let her down when she most urgently needed them. Was someone there or not? Who? But at least as long as this irritation with herself held its place she was able to retain some control, keep the dread in proportion. This, after all, was grey matter kicking back against panic, the way her parents had taught her. They always said a cool head would bring her through almost any difficulty. Rationality they adored. But, opposed to the coolness, Megan was aware of her eyes and intuition ganging up and insisting this imprecise figure was undoubtedly the fur-collar man from the train. Her brain said no, and again no – said there had been nothing like such clarity and that, in any case, he had left the train at Dobecross. She saw this illogical wish to identify as similar to how she had felt haunted by the yellow VW in London. All het-up fancy, wasn't it, maybe understandable in her nervy, adulterous state, but foolish, just the same, surely?

And so she was able to chart not too badly the frontier between what she felt and what she knew. What she felt was what anyone might feel in a spot like this and at this hour on discovering a secret observer close: it brought her near to collapse. On the other hand, what she knew via her thinking mind was . . . was that she did not know even one little thing for sure – not who, what or whether, and – above all – not why, and that her feelings might be absurd, contemptible.

One tactic Megan's mind prescribed at once was to resist peering too hard towards whatever it might be and, instead, drag out the process of transferring and settling the carrier bags in the car and seem preoccupied. If she stared, showed she was aware, it might provoke a rush of action by him. She fixed on the notion that there would be no attack until she went to the driver's door to get in. This was why she lingered on the passenger side. He knew her car? Waiting for her there was schemed? Never mind: the car might be what he homed on, but it was also a physical defence, a happy lump of metal, a rampart. It sat there, small but beautifully obstructive between them. She reckoned that only if she made him switch plans by revealing she had seen him would he try something right away.

Yes, yes, she realized that in the few seconds she messed about with the last two carrier bags she had dropped her supposed uncertainties. Someone *was* there, it *was* a he, and the face she clearly pictured when gazing terrified into the depths of the Astra's luggage space was the fur collar's. Some fraction of her asserted that this shift in her reactions was pathetic, feeble. It had become a minor, unimportant fraction now, though, and shrinking.

She could formulate her first problem very easily. When she closed the tailgate, it would be the obvious – only – routine procedure to go from behind the car to the driver's side ready to depart. How else to drive home? Or, it would be the obvious – only – routine procedure if this were a normal car park situation and she had not done her battle analysis and decided the Astra was her main, possibly only, protection. So, for tonight, to move to the driver's door might in fact not be the obvious and only sequence, but suicidal. It would entail standing still for at least a moment or two on his side, her back to the threat, bent over, eyes intent on finding the door keyhole without delay and unable to look out for him. But she would have to move in her chosen direction very soon. And if she went pointlessly back to the passenger side this would be as much a give-away as if she stared. It would show she had spotted him and was seeking cover behind the car. Would he come at a gallop? What if he did? Might he only want to speak to her? Did people wait hidden in car parks in the middle of the night for a nice chat-up? Maybe not. She could not fiddle with these parcels much longer, or that itself would be a sign she was alarmed.

What if she simply galloped for cover herself? Leave the tailgate high, so he was not warned the operation had finished, and hurtle up the path towards the station and help. She thought she had seen one uniformed railway worker when they came in. Of course she had. This was a main-line station, for God's sake. There had to be staff around, even so late, and possibly rail police. She might try that. It became, then, a matter of measuring the distance by eye and working out the chances of being caught before she reached the lights at the footbridge and could get herself heard, and possibly seen – assuming there were someone to hear and see. Her car was about half way into the parking ground. She had, say, fifty yards of that to cross, then another good fifty yards along the narrow path between the railway lines and the high-walled rear yards to offices. On the rail side of the path was a tall, strong, safety fence. Once she was into that path she would be enclosed and able only to go forward, like a rat in a lab run.

If she reached the bridge she might be all right, because it was lit and she would be all-round visible. Surely an attack there would be too risky. Across the bridge there were telephones in the station and she would reach Colin, if Colin were home. In ten minutes he could be here. Was it bad, disgusting, to expect his aid now, when she intended saying a permanent goodbye? But he was still her husband, and a big cop husband, and if you were menaced where else could you call? Marriage meant something, even this one. If he did turn out, would she still be able to give him the quit message tonight? If she did not tell him tonight, would she ever? She would decide about that when she had to, definitely not now.

There were choices. She could close the tailgate, then move swiftly with her key ready to the driver's door and hope to get in, lock it again from inside, and have the car going and away at once, before he could interfere. Sometimes the E Astra started instantly, even in cold weather. Or, she could climb into the back now among the carrier bags, then over the rear seats to the wheel. This had the advantage that the doors would not need to be unlocked at all. But the tailgate would probably have to stay open. Could you lock it from inside? Would there be time? Could he fling himself in behind her?

And, as she raised her hand to pull the tailgate slowly down, she decided. She would not run, and she would not hurl herself into the back among the pressies. She must go fast to the driver's door and hope to be rolling before anyone could even reach the car. Because of where he stood, she would be driving away from him, not past him. How could he harm her if everything was locked? And then that deeper query: why did he want to harm her? Rape? He would follow someone from London for that? It would be almost flattering. Crazy, though. Not rape, just an attack. Why, then? Yes, why? This was something to do with Tambo? Something to do with Colin? Something to do with the mucky power-game jobs they had? Something to do with the VW? She drew the tailgate down and locked it.

This plan of getting to the driver's door appealed most to her because somewhere she still had the conviction, minor but hopeful, that there was nobody among the trees at all. This had to be the probability, and her parents had insisted she always look for probabilities, though, of course, without wholly excluding the aberrant. Thus, it would be farcical to scramble in through the tailgate, all legs and arms and breathlessness, and idiotic to hare towards the footbridge if nobody pursued her. She recalled an ancient joke about two girls walking past an army camp and one saying, 'I've got a terrible feeling we're not being followed.'

And if nobody did come after her, would she have the guts at the bridge to decide there definitely had not been an observer and return to the Astra? If she did not have the guts and called Colin out, she felt sure, on second thoughts, that she would be unable to do what she had finally built herself up to do: tell him their marriage was over. *Thanks for the rescue, Galahad, and incidentally I'm fucking off for keeps.* Low, yes, disgusting. In fact, impossible. As she moved towards the driver's door she did glance again at where she believed the watcher to be and was positive now it had been an error. Plenty of shadows, plenty of jostling, waving branches, no prowler. Just Nature. Perhaps an eye mistake, through two layers of unclean Astra glass. God, she giggled to herself, I might have been clambering madly over the goods and seats or trying for a rapid hobble in heels up that dark, hemmed-in track.

Chapter 24

Arriving at the station for her London trip, Megan had been unable to find a parking spot any nearer to the platforms. She was late and could have done with a shorter walk. This parking place and a few others near by were marked out not by white lines but slightly raised bricks on three sides. You felt you were parking on a gravestone. All it needed was a few flowers. *Strew on the oil leaks, roses*. At least, though, this space was not right up against the restless trees of the perimeter. She disliked those places. Cars there were more liable to visits by thieves or louts, because they could get to your vehicle and away from it under cover. Also, late at night, with few people around, she found the special darkness of the trees eerie. That was shaming, really – childishly fanciful, a throw-back to fairy tales set in wicked woods.

She had paid, locked up, walked quickly across the car park and then along the narrow ash-track path towards the footbridge. Once she reached the end of the path she always felt her London trip had really started. For its fifty or so yards, she was conscious of being almost claustrophobically enclosed, high fence on one side, high walls on the other. During a science programme on TV she had seen laboratory rats directed down a wired-in run for some experiment, and she sympathized. Then, though, just before the footbridge, the walls ended. At the same point, the path ceased to hug the rail lines and the fence veered away. Suddenly, the path broadened out into a wide quadrangle. Release. Invariably, she felt here that rush of excited freedom, the sense of scope and range, which the prospect of London unfailingly gave her. She loved the sheer size of London and all its opportunities and brilliant

assets – theatre, cinema, magnificent shops, galleries, restaurants. Today, they planned to see the controversial movie
JFK. It would almost certainly appear soon at one of the local
cinemas, but viewing it in London would somehow be more
an experience, and not just because the ticket cost double. She
liked telling people back here that she hoped to catch this or
that film or play in the West End, especially controversial ones.
It showed you were right up with current debate. London
folk did speak of *catching* shows – their lives were so full
and active.

Now and then she wondered whether Tambo seemed special
because he, too, was part of this sparkling London scene. After
all, he accompanied her to the cinemas, theatres, galleries and
restaurants. And, although he lived in what he told her was a
very ordinary flat in a very ordinary street between Highbury
and Islington, they never went anywhere so grubby. Instead,
they originally used a modest but nice little hotel in South
Kensington, and now he had the run of an opulent apartment
in the smartest section of Mayfair. So, her days and occasional
nights with Tambo had become glamorous. But whenever she
asked herself if this explained his attraction – and she asked
herself, often – she could answer that things started long
before he moved to the Met. London was a nice extra but only
an extra.

In any case, once in a while she had the impression of
something unpleasant, even dangerous, about to burst through
the glamour. The gloss could suddenly look – well, look like
nothing but gloss. At an Impressionist exhibition in Piccadilly
a few months ago Tambo had suddenly come up to her and
said they must leave immediately, offering no reason. And
even afterwards he had never given a reason that convinced
her. They had only just managed to get into the gallery after
queuing for an hour, yet he insisted they go at once. He was
very tense, looked almost sick, looked suddenly very bent and
beaten and old. At first, she thought it was to do with their
affair – that in the crowd he had spotted someone it would
embarrass him to see while with her. That could happen. He
was properly divorced, though, so why the anxiety? In any
case, the intensity of it seemed too much. She drew back from

attributing physical fear to men like Tambo, or like Colin, come to that, and so she still picked other, milder terms to describe Tambo's appearance that day: tense, sick, bent, beaten, old. In fact, she knew now and had known then that he seemed terrified. When he grabbed her arm and shoved her towards the exit, she had been gazing at *The Suicide* by Manet, and she was so shocked by the change in him that for weeks afterwards, and very occasionally even now, she would glimpse again for a moment the grim detail of that painting whenever Tambo touched her: the white-faced blood-stained corpse stretched out on a bed and holding a pistol in the right hand. Eventually, Tambo offered the tale that he had seen his ex-wife with two of her sisters and had to avoid such a family gang. It did not wash. You grew used to bleak mysteries if your lover or your husband was police, but they were mysteries that scarred. Perhaps what it came down to was you went to the man who scarred you least, and Colin had been at it longer and in many more ways.

The train had been crowded, mainly with parties of shoppers. Megan hoped she would not see anyone she knew. She could do without talk about Colin, children, schools, domesticity, Christmas. For today she was no part of all that. Yes, she would bring back presents, but she wanted to feel she was on her own, leading that other life. When she arrived in London, Tambo would be waiting, and would hang back until the rest of the passengers dispersed. It was furtive, but one of the conditions you accepted and grew used to.

She had managed to find a seat and hid herself behind a book.

Chapter 25

Jack Lamb and Harpur had a range of alternative rendezvous points for use when Jack wanted to say something. Harpur always let him specify. A detective did let his grass specify venues. It was the grass's body, and mere courtesy said he picked where to risk it. Harpur needed Lamb safe – ran a career on his survival. No other informant could touch him for amount or reliability. Megan despised these skills, thought detection should be what she called 'open'. Once or twice, years ago, Harpur had tried to explain Lamb's underhand magnificence to her, but it was like praising snot to a hanky.

Jill took the call from him today and came to tell Harpur in the kitchen. 'One of your touts, Dad.'

'Who?'

'Touts have names? But definitely a grass voice. I recognized it. He's called here before. Sounds as if he knows about Mum. It was that same voice, but oilier, vicary – for the sympathy bit?'

'Did he mention her?' Harpur asked.

'They don't mention anything, do they, except how to reach you? Hazel's found some pictures and stuff.'

When Harpur picked up the phone, Lamb said: 'Col, I can skip commiserations?'

'Of course.'

'You know the regret's there.'

'Of course.'

'Megan loathed me.'

'Certainly.'

'But you know it's there, just the same.'

'Of course.'

'Thanks, Col. We could meet?'

'Of course.'

'The cannon park?'

'Certainly.'

'In an hour?'

'Great.'

'There's an ironical slant to this, Col.'

'Really?'

'She despised my activities, yet they could help find who did it.'

'She prized irony.'

'Education. But no help against a knife. Col, regrettably I have to bring you some painful intimacies. I'm hearing nothing from this end, but there are London signals, roundabout some of them, others tangible.'

'What's that mean?'

But this had already been a long telephone call for Jack and he put the receiver down.

What Jack called the cannon park were overgrown concrete emplacements for Second World War anti-aircraft guns on high wooded ground just outside the town. Lamb liked these bits of military history, and they also sometimes met at a foreshore blockhouse from which the Home Guard would have tried to throw back Hitler's invasion. He used to stand at an observation slit there, gazing out fixedly across the mud flats and brown sea, as if sorry the Germans had failed to show, and sorry he was born too late for battle. Harpur went into the sitting-room to join the girls until it was time to leave.

Jill said: 'If we're going to Iles's place for Christmas we'll have to take presents.'

'Get something for the baby,' Hazel said.

'Yes,' Harpur replied. 'And some wine.'

'Wine? You? Will Iles keep a straight face?' Jill asked.

'I'll spend, don't worry. It will be something fine.'

'You mean right up to £3.50?' Hazel asked. 'As to whether Scott comes it's tricky,' Hazel replied.

'There's his sort of mother and our sort,' Jill said.

'She's turning Scott nervy,' Hazel replied. 'I might ditch him.'

'For God's sake be a bit more humane,' Jill shouted. 'He's only a kid still.'

'I don't need that kind of kid.'

Harpur said: 'I'll get Desmond Iles to meet her. He'll have her eating out of his hand.'

'At least,' Jill replied.

Hazel said: 'This him, Dad?' She had what looked like some photographs in her hand and held up a couple.

'Who?' Harpur replied. He was sitting on the far side of the room, near but not at Megan's desk. He felt more comfortable like that.

'The London one. He looks quite sensitive. Perhaps it's the sweetest two pix out of two hundred.' She brought them over. They were four-by-sixes of Tambo in a mauve sweatshirt, one head-on, the other half profile, doing very well by his nose. You could see why he might fancy himself at amateur dramatics.

'Yes, there was a reasonable side to him,' Harpur said.

'Slippery, I'd say,' Jill stated.

'A bit,' Harpur replied.

'What else? He *is* police, Dad, and climbing the ladder,' Hazel said.

'Where did you get them?' Harpur asked. 'I don't want you going through her desk.'

'Iles and Garland did,' Hazel said.

'Routine,' Harpur replied.

'No, they were hidden in *Money*,' Hazel said.

'Whose?'

'A novel,' Hazel replied. 'I was wondering about what you said – books having some point. I mean, that coming from *you*. So I pulled out the one with the most fetching title, to give it a whirl.'

'*Money*, yes.'

'No, the one next to it, same bloke: *Dead Babies*. Then I saw *Money* was sort of swollen. Inflated? There were letters, too. Yes, cagey.'

'Better not read them, Dad,' Jill said. 'Graphic the word?'

'Should Iles see them?' Hazel asked.

'Possibly,' Harpur replied. He prepared to set out for the

cannon park. Harpur often wondered whether two big men talking in these remote spots were more noticeable than if they had chatted casually in a pub. He never said so to Lamb, though, because Jack ruled on geography. It might have helped if Lamb were less conspicuous. Harpur was big enough – had heard himself described as a fair Rocky Marciano – but Lamb made him look frail and stunted. Another factor: although Jack fussed over meeting places and feared telephone lines, he loved bizarre, memorable, expensive clothes, frequently real rainbow jobs. Probably he wanted to knock off a decade or two in the eyes of his live-in teenage girlfriend, Helen. Why not?

Jill said: 'Nothing in the letters about her quitting us.'

'She'd never have gone,' Harpur replied.

'Honestly, Dad? You honestly believe it?' Jill asked.

'Don't you want to read them?' Hazel said.

'Not much. I had the résumé,' Harpur replied.

Today at the gun site, Lamb had on what looked like navy blue jodhpurs and calf-high black boots under a cavalry style beige bum-freezer overcoat. Sometimes at these army spots he liked to wear items in tune, and had once arrived in a beret with a Montgomery badge up. Harpur parked some way from the gun positions and walked, but Lamb brought his Lancia close. It was cold and growing dark.

'Colin, this lad Megan was seeing in London – not too clean?'

'Tambo? I know nothing against him.'

'Nothing except he was—'

'Nothing professional,' Harpur said.

They strolled around the emplacements as they talked. Lamb now and then throwing an arm up like the barrel of a gun and with his mouth making Bofors noises against ghost Heinkels. Maybe he yearned like many for the plain dangers and heroics of old wars, so different from the devious perils he lived with now. And then there were also the simple, uncalculating comradeships of war, not the back-scratch dependency he and Harpur had. Lamb said: 'Well, true, Tambo seemed to stay above board while he was here. I never heard anything definite.'

'Most of us would settle for that.'

'Too modest, Col. But since he's up there – different pressures, different opportunities, bigger opportunities? Plus costs. Bigger costs? A divorce and so on. This is what I mean about signals.'

'From?'

'London.'

'Yes, but where in London? Who? What status information?'

Lamb opened up again on the raiding bombers. 'They shall not pass.'

'Wrong war.' You did not ask Lamb about the status of his information and expect an answer. He himself was its status. But Harpur had not realized Lamb could call on such high-level sources in London, and this half excused the rudeness of enquiring.

'Tambo could be in someone's pocket, Col. *Is* in someone's pocket. All that training in integrity you gave here, and this happens the moment he hits the capital. A destructive place.'

'Megan adored it.'

Lamb put a heavy arm across Harpur's shoulders, as though wanting to say something, but reluctant.

'You mean she was drawn into something there, Jack?'

'Oh, not that she knew, not at all. Megan would be appalled, I'm sure,' Lamb replied.

'But she was drawn in?'

'Closeness to police. It's always problematical, isn't it? People standing close also catch the shit.'

'My daughter's boyfriend's mother thinks so.'

Again Lamb appeared unwilling to speak. Then he said: 'Col, as I understand it, there are tapes. That's what I meant, tangible.'

'Who? Megan on tapes? With him?'

Christ, letters, now this. The letters had scarcely interested him, because they were Tambo, not her. The tapes would be different.

'This is the tip as it comes to me, Col.'

'Who'd do it? How?'

Jack nodded the huge head to show these doubts were

reasonable. 'One of his favours – the use of a flat. That's what I was saying: painful, delicate. Do I want to be the one to bring this sort of information, these rough glimpses? Look, I feel tainted by it.' His voice went down, clobbered by sorrow and self-pity. 'That's how she saw me, yes – tainted?'

'Along those lines, Jack. She had some very fixed ideas.'

'And she taught the daughters similar. I don't blame her. Or not much. Even today I heard it in that child's tone. Jill? Yet there's no progress without some dirty insights by my sort, is there?'

'You're not a sort. You're one-off, Jack. Unfortunately.'

'Kind, Col.'

A bit of snow was flicking their faces and they sheltered against the concrete outer wall of one of the emplacements. Harpur felt unsure whether it was the cold or shock, but his mind seemed slow. 'Jack, all this trouble – I mean, seeking London information. What's—'

'In it for me? We help each other, don't we, you and I, Col? We go a long way back. All right, Megan hated the arrangement and—'

'She didn't know much about it.'

'Enough to hate it and me. But the arrangement survived that, still survives, I hope. So, how could I ignore your plight, Col? I hear the funeral was exactly right.'

'What flat, Jack? They went out to his place in North London. Highbury?'

'He's got something there, yes. They never used it. This wasn't Highbury. Palatial. Kitted out to impress. All kinds entertained there. Mayfair. Company owned, according to the street list. I might do some director tracing.'

'And the place is bugged?' Harpur said.

'Possibly to eavesdrop on so-called business guests. Taittinger. Always replenished. Frozen meals.'

'Fish?' Harpur asked.

'Why?'

'Megan wouldn't like a luxury pad like that. She'd sense something wrong.'

'Like she did with me,' Lamb said.

'And me.'

'She put up with it. I mean, from him, Col.'

'Perhaps he had something special. There's a mauve sweatshirt.'

'Excuse me, Colin, but look at it this way, she's getting older.'

'Moral certainties fade? Not in her parents, and she's like them.'

'Excuse me again, Colin, but they don't live with a cop, so haven't suffered this slow smashing of scruples.'

'Ah, I see what you mean.'

'Almost all of us – we get older, we trim to the dear old world. Why Christ quit in time at thirty-three. By Megan's age a woman is starting to wonder how much longer she'll catch the eye. They grow less exacting.'

Harpur stumbled over one of the metal rails on which ammunition trolleys must have moved. 'You've got these bastard tapes, haven't you, Jack?'

'Up in London for one day only, who wants to trek out to Highbury? Accepting a handier venue would be only good sense.'

'Tambo in whose pocket, Jack?'

'But he's possibly struggling to climb out. To get wholesome again. That's the buzz. I think it's very credible. Now, trying to dismantle that kind of alliance can be hazardous, obviously, Col – to him and his. People who've invested grandly in a well-placed officer are dead upset if he suddenly turns his back. They'd want to stick some pressure on him, yes? And this is someone whose wife and kids have gone. So where to look if they mean to give a heavy warning, but not damage the actual asset? You know how they think. Didn't something like it nearly happen to Denise when people wanted to damage you? Of course it did. They look at his lover, if you don't mind the word, Col.'

'Who says he's struggling to get free?'

'Again pardon me if I speak out of turn. Let's consider this. We have a long-established relationship here, yes – him, Megan? Suppose he wanted it more serious with her. Suppose he wanted her to go to him permanently.'

'Impossible.'

111

'Which? That he'd want it or that Megan would go?'

'That. The last.'

'Of course it's impossible. But we don't need the second, only the first. If he was trying to persuade her, Col, he'd realize straight off that Megan would never agree while he was supping payola. Anyone could diagnose that in her character, and he's more than anyone. So, he's trying to break loose, looking for the road sign, Probity. And the people who've bought him soon realize why he's doing it. Col, they'd be monitoring him, wouldn't they? The tapes are only part of it. This is someone they've poured funds into. He belongs to them. That's how they'd see it. He can't go offering himself to somebody else. They won't let his love-life spoil things. People at Tambo's rank are hard to net. Answer – take out Megan and you take out the cop's silly nostalgia for purity.'

Harpur said: 'Trying to break loose, yet still using the donated flat?'

'He'd know it would be provocative just to walk away. He's running things down slowly. Spurning the flat might come last.'

'I'll hear the tapes, Jack.'

Lamb went into a clipped, evasive, boardroom voice. 'I'd rather not disclose at this stage who his paymaster is. I say at this stage. Perhaps subsequently, yes. You might find you could not resist taking some action, and that would point the finger my way and my source's way. I have to see ramifications. These people know how to reach out, Col. But, my God, do I need to tell you? They've done it to Megan.'

'How? How did they do it, Jack?'

'Oh, deputed someone, I should think. An outfit like this would have a nominal director for rough assignments.'

'Fur collar? Moustache? Twenties?'

Growing restless, Lamb had stepped out from the bit of cover and was standing in a swirl of snow, huge and blurred, like a cliff or furniture van. People thought of grasses as small, foxy. People could be wrong. Megan said once that when she visualized what she termed 'police spies' it was as the writer George Orwell described them in some famous book about

112

the Spanish Civil War – unkempt, sleazy, furtive. None of that was Jack, and she knew it. Always Lamb gave Harpur heart.

'You're ahead of me, Col – as so often. What *is* this?'

'Someone thinks she was travelling back with a man like that. It might be a mistake. Perhaps not *with* him. Just being dogged by him.'

'Yes, those could be hit tactics. Sorry – I'm telling you your business: they do the thing at a distance, so enquiries are distant, too. Iles and his crew have heard of this man?'

'I've heard of him.'

'This could be helpful. Can we get a fuller description? You have one already?' He rejoined Harpur, snow piled up loose on his hair like froth on a pint.

'I'll hear the tapes.' Harpur said. 'Why you brought the car close? They must have cost you. Look, I—'

'Couldn't come near to finding that sort of cash yourself. Of course you couldn't. We look after each other, Col. Don't I know I can rely on reciprocity when due? It satisfies me to be perhaps putting things to rights for Megan by methods she thought ill of, possibly did not understand properly.' He shook snow from the bum-freezer, giving its beigeness more chance. 'No, I haven't got the tapes.'

'Fuck you, Jack,' he bellowed. 'I don't believe that.' He grabbed at Lamb's arm and tried to swing him around so they were face to face. It was like trying to shift a battleship by handling the mooring rope.

In his own time, Lamb did turn to face him, though. 'How would I have them, Col? People are going to part with such material?'

'Copies, for God's sake. Why else are you talking about cost?'

The clouds had gone over and there was no more snow. In the improved light Harpur could see solid grief and eternal, healthy wiliness in Lamb's vast face. 'What I've managed to lay hands on, Col – and this was tricky – trickier than anything else I've ever done – I've got hold of a transcript. What was said between them was written down for me, for us. There seemed to be two visits to the place that day. The bugging apparatus gives a time note. Afternoon, late evening. She must

113

have hurried for the last train afterwards. You're welcome to read it in the car. I can't let you take the papers away. Why I drove close, yes.'

'Meaning you've edited things.' Harpur said at once. 'Supposed to be kindness. You don't want me listening first hand to their—'

'To their intimacies?'

'The ecstasy shouts. The gasping. She's into all that.'

'There are spoken intimacies written down, believe me, Col. Why I said painful to bring this.'

'Jack, I've got to hear all of it.'

'Keep your voice down. You'll scare the voles and warrior spirits. No, Col, this is just a reading job.'

'You want to be one-up by knowing more than me, you sod. Information in the bank. Typical soiled fink tactics. Megan was bloody right.'

'You're overwrought. Agony's made you savage. Come on.'

They walked to the Lancia. Lamb sat bent forward over the wheel. 'Fink. Thanks. You hurt, Col. You'll get no overlord's name from me, nor the Mayfair address, though obviously I've got it, by my own methods – fink methods. I've even set a couple of lads watching it now and then, tracing where those associated with the place go. All that stays private to me – stays valuable to me, cosy, like you say.' He put a cassette into the player. 'But as to what goes on at the address? All right, so hear the bloody lot from this fink then.'

Chapter 26

Always when her train drew into London on these trips, Megan had a mixed rush of feelings. Among them was a foul, vivid sense of dread. The first time she experienced this it dazed her. Since then, she had worked out some kind of explanation, but was still astonished. All that pleasurable rubbish about scope, range, freedom, opportunity, seemed to turn tail as she looked from her carriage window on to the station. It happened now. For a couple of seconds, she felt conscious of nothing but dirt and threat.

She saw why: it was the realization she really knew nothing at all about this town – what she called in her mind at these moments 'Tambo's London'. When she was at home, or just emerging from that rat-run station path, London *did* look like all those delicious, big-deal items, plus love, sex, fun. From that distance, it also looked like the friendly but thrilling place her parents had taught her to delight in as a child and young woman. Of course, she had always known this was a carefully choosy way of seeing it. She also knew London had changed and was changing: was growing darker. And sometimes, during these grand days with Tambo she thought she had tiny glimpses into that darkness, and knew she caught a whiff of rottenness from hidden and unmentionable corners, but very close. That day at the Impressionists would do for a start. At home she occasionally felt much the same about the behaviour of Colin and Iles and Jack Lamb and Erogenous and Francis Garland – in fact about all that local mesh, except possibly the Chief himself. In London, for those opening moments each time, it seemed worse. London was bigger. London would be crueller, viler. More meant worse. She saw this collapse went beyond pessimism and into despair.

Well, you could not live in despair, and by the time the train actually stopped, she had always compelled herself to chuck the mood. Glancing about for Tambo now and praying he would not be in that fucking mauve sweatshirt she pigeon-holed despair and got a good smile up: began convincing herself again that what she smelled was not corruption but salt of the earth humanity in big numbers.

She had her methods of climbing back to high spirits: her parents had always stressed one had a duty not to stay miser-able – 'down' as they called it. As soon as she met Tambo she would plunge into the kind of talk impossible at home with Colin: interesting, stimulating intellectual talk she thought of as special to her and Tambo, and special to the London setting. Damn it, she came here for a culture treat, among other things, not a fright palsy.

As she bubbled on now, Megan studied his face, scared that as well as the beams of welcome and glints of fine appetite she might see signs of that appalling terror he showed in the art gallery. Today, though, he seemed all right; eyes steady, voice relaxed, no new stress lines. As far as she could make out, he was not wearing the mauve thing under his overcoat. Tambo looked like someone who would do his talented best to keep this vast city wholesome, the way she so badly wanted it – wholesome but still fun. He was the sort of man she could, did, love. When she felt like this, the apparent craziness of losing faith in one cop and turning to another was easy to understand, because this cop was as cops should be: honour-able, transparent, strong, capable, his soul untrampled by the job. He would not turn villain to fight villainy. She could link her life to a life like this and find joy in the move. That did not mean, though, she was ready now, today, to say she would come to him. But the option was very much there, attractive and pressing.

God, she wished they didn't have to use that creepy, rich flat. On the other hand, she did not much like the idea of going to his place in North London. For one thing, it was marginally but unredeemably the wrong part of North London. Also, it would bring a tinge of domesticity, and she was not ready for that. Not with him. She had plenty.

The shops put her at ease. She loved their warmth, refined odour and carpeting. Quality goods could always thrill and uplift Megan. They declared that people did care about well-made things, that taste still counted. And, by spending on such items, one backed this excellence, became a part of it. There was stature in the passage of money. One had all sorts of needs. A metropolis could provide.

In the flat, they always left the champagne untouched for the first hour or two. This was so important. It kept their obligations low, at least for now. A roof and the bed were enough, and occasionally not even the bed. In the past, they had made love on the floor. They had made love standing in the kitchen, rattling the good, shelved china. She liked it standing – youthful, athletic, like kids in a back lane. In any case she did not want her senses fuddled by complimentary fine wine, nor his. As they took their clothes off and said how they had longed for each other, and yelled and hissed what they meant to do to each other, the words had to be well-chosen, clear, gloriously precise. They both enjoyed shouting, before, during. Or, at least, Tambo made out he liked it – maybe to humour her: she did not care. Megan saw it as her way of defying the smug ambience of this apartment block. She wanted other occupants made uneasy by the squawks of delight, wanted them disgusted if possible. It would satisfy her to be overheard. There were moments when she even hoped she and Tambo had been seen arriving and people could put faces to this hearty, hungry, indecent din, and especially *her* face.

Not all of this was coarse and anatomical, though perhaps she got most from that. 'Your body's made for me,' he said. 'So, why isn't it mine?'

'It is.'

'Today.'

'We have a lot of todays.'

'We have *some* todays.'

'We make the most of them.'

'Could we make the most of them if they were always? That what you're scared of, Megan?'

'I'm not scared. Do I act scared, feel scared?'

117

'You feel full of it.'

'Boasting again. But, yes, I am.'

Afterwards, the champagne, a little quarrel about freezer meals, then more love and a dash to a restaurant and a dash back to more love, more good chat, some brilliant shouting. Taking the freezer meals, so his benefactor would not seem snubbed, pissed her off, and she spelled it out. This was what she meant: such sudden glimpses into something secret and doubtful, right on top of those bright episodes of fierce happiness.

Chapter 27

Jill took another call. 'It's Roger, Dad,' she said, hand over the mouthpiece, 'of Roger and Coral. Dim eminences from mum's Fortnightly? Remember?'

He took the receiver. 'Colin? Rog. On the train with Megan? The fish man? Look, do tell me to get lost if you feel like it, and I'll totally understand and so will Coral. But we thought we should somehow do the traditional Christmas Fortnightly. One feels Megan would want that. Obviously, not in your home. We'll stage it here. All a bit hurried. Everyone I've spoken to has agreed and we're running it tonight. Traditional Thursday. Perhaps you think the whole business pretentious wind-bagging, but several members suggested, and Coral and I wholeheartedly agree, that we should invite you along.'

'This is a kindness, Roger.'

'Tongue in cheek? It's the least we can do. However, it's what I meant – tell us to drop dead if you like, it not being your scene, and so on, and why should it be, for Heaven's sake, a cabal of book-jerks? But we do hope you can come, even at short notice. The form these Christmas things take, and which we'll observe for her sake, is much more relaxed than our usual sessions. No speaker, as such. Some drinks and snacks, perhaps one or two of us reading our own works, a little discussion, then more drinks. I might do my poem, for instance, which I hope didn't fall entirely flat with you.'

'Not at all. Full of, well, mood.'

'Mood? Yes. That's gracious of you.'

'Poetry not usually being up my street.'

'Without wishing to patronize, Colin, poetry is not for poets, but for readers – all readers. So, I'd be very thrilled to hear your unjargonized, straight comments in discussion, believe me. We're frank with one another, though humane, I trust. At around eight o'clock here.'

'Grand.'

'Is this preposterous – but did that fish lead anywhere, or Coral's theories about the fur collar man, if you don't mind my bringing up these painful matters?'

'Nothing in either, I'm afraid, Rog. But—'

'I feel absurd now, parcelling up a bit of cod or whatever.'

'Both might have mattered. One never knows. I'm grateful.'

'Obviously, we are as much amateurs in detection as you are – or say you are – in poetry. Yet a terrible event like this draws all sorts together. It's the one positive aspect, possibly.'

'I hadn't thought of it like that.'

When Roger rang off, Harpur went to the kitchen and tipped the waste bin out again but could not find the poem. He realized that the small bag lining the bin would have been changed by one of the girls and put into the plastic sack ready to go out. Three other bags were also in the sack and he had to empty two of these before spotting the crumpled poem. By then he had a good quantity of rubbish on the floor. The poem was a little stained by baked beans liquor, but in fair shape and he sponged it clean with the dish cloth and smoothed out the sheet. He read the lines on the draining board and found them interesting in their way. Jill came out and read the poem with him. 'It's good,' she said. 'Gets you here.' She punched the pit of her stomach. She and Harpur replaced the debris and he swabbed the lino once more.

'I need to mug up on Roger's work. They're doing a memorial Fortnightly. I can't decently dodge it,' Harpur said.

'Of course you can't. They'll have two minutes' silence?'

'If they can manage it.'

'You want to take the ashes?' She glanced up. Temporarily, they were on top of the store cupboard in the *Smiley's People* video box until Harpur got an urn.

'They didn't ask me to, so no.'

Roger and Coral had a distinguished old stone house at the edge of the city, with flagged floors in part, and several useful antiques and respectable water colours. Between them, beneath it all, there must be some genuine taste, or perhaps the whole lot was inherited. He arrived at the same time as Avril Yane, who had given that superb cremation address, and parked his ancient Ford behind her blue Passat. She seemed to see something warm in that nearness and gripped his arm for a moment at the doorway. Inside, the party had hit its stride, with plenty of wine and whisky, and what had to be an authentic jazz magnifico wailing away on tape.

After a while, Harpur again had the impression that Avril would like deeper communion, and she seemed to feel franker about it now the funeral had gone. Avril was bright, vigorous and pretty for her age, still able to look the part in denim, and a fine public speaking voice, but Harpur did not really need anything closer with her, whatever the cars signalled. They drank wine together and he chatted, trying to keep things impersonal, safe and off the literary. In a while he saw that, half stewed or not, she felt his indifference and had begun to grow evil, her voice now throaty, hard, jealous.

'What is it, then, Colin, lovey, you still yearn for her?'

'Of course. It's no time, is it?'

'Oh, sure.' She swigged some of her wine. 'Look, don't you know she meant to leave you?' She took a refill. 'You must have heard of the thing with Tambo? Far, far be it from me to dirty Megan's image, Col, but I can't believe I'm telling you anything new.'

'A friendship – books. Never more, and it just faded when he left.'

'Bollocks, if I may say.'

'Look, I ought to get around and see a few people – thank them for honouring Megan.'

'Why do you think she flitted to London so often?'

'Her kind of place. Mind stuff.'

'She went to see him. Panting.'

'I'm going to speak to Maurice. It is Maurice, isn't it – the post-deconstructionalist clergyman?'

'Megan's talked to me about this, for God's sake,' Avril replied, booming. 'I was her best friend, wasn't I? Why shut your eyes and ears to it all, Colin? Idiotic question – because of the children, obviously. You'll screw the stopper down on

121

it all now. You ask, why do needless injury to them? They loved her, and you want they go on loving her, esteeming her. Fine. But, also, why lie to yourself, and why switch yourself off emotionally, dear Col, like some Spanish widow?' She touched his lapel in that fond, feverish way of hers again, spilling wine on his shoe.

'They might have done some theatre in London together. That sort of thing?'

'Listen: I'm reporting this not to hurt her, but for your own, oh, I don't know – your emancipation. Get out from under the grief, Col – it's too much. She's actually told me, and more than once, she'd leave you. I can say it straight out only because she also said she knew you sensed this, maybe even the kids, too. True? Yes. Megan thought you'd be all right, you were always drifting round, anyway, looking for newness. And now you stop drifting around? Because she's dead? That makes sense? You're in shock, perhaps? Or don't I suit? Go on, say so if that's what you think. Too old? Too heavy? Thanks very much indeed, Colin.'

'Avril, you're certainly—'

'Theatre? Culture? They had use of a flat up there. A plush love nest, Colin. I don't say no arty outings, but this was the centre piece.'

'Impossible.'

'Ah, you know about it? As a matter of fact, it sickened her a bit, but not enough. She spoke about the place with contempt, sure it was some sort of dab in the hand. Once in an outburst of disgust she actually intoned the whole damnable address to me, like a curse. Or a millstone. Mayfair. Street. Number. I could give it to you, but won't – a confidence. But you see what I mean?'

Coral approached in scarlet sweater and black leather mini and Harpur wondered again whether Roger could cope: 'This looks easily the most animated discussion in the room,' she said. 'Can anyone join in?'

'Oh, just should Rushdie re-recant?' Harpur replied.

Roger climbed on to a nice Victorian high-backed chair and spoke 'Invigilation' in what Harpur considered just the right throw-away style. He switched to whisky: not his drink, but he saw no gin or cider. Then a very young dark-haired girl with winning skin and legs and lips and poise read what seemed to be a parable sonnet about the benefits in returning cans to collection points for aluminium scrap. Afterwards there was free discussion of the two works. Harpur required his number made with the dark-haired girl and asked her whether she worked to a timetable or by inspiration. She said she would have to think that one over, and he took this as rosy, meaning further contact.

'Oh, so you fancied that, did you?' Avril snarled quietly, as soon as discussion ended. 'Well, get this, chief super dick, she's young and lovely and slim, yes, but gay as bunting.'

'Had her?' Harpur replied.

'Possibly. She's not interested in some cuckolded widower.'

'Oh, still that? Cuckolded where, then, for God's sake?'

'You really can't believe it, can you, Col, poor blind love?'

'No, I simply can't. I knew Megan.'

'Not alone, Colin. All right: 26A Careen Street, W1. Convinced, damn it? Would I make up something so specific? Would she?'

First Lamb now Avril: he was getting good at sucking stuff from people, even if sucking it brought agony. He left his car and found a cab, scared Avril might do an unidentified spite call to headquarters about an old Granada, the driver four times over. When he reached home, Jack Lamb's companion, Helen Surtees, was there with the girls and Scott and Darren, coaching them in ballet steps, while whistling some slab of the classics.

'Helen has to see you, Dad,' Hazel said. 'She's been waiting.'

'About Jack,' Helen said. She looked very troubled. Even drunk, Harpur could tell that.

They stopped the dancing.

'I think it's private,' Jill said.

Harpur took Helen into the kitchen and closed the door. There was still a slight sweet smell from the spilled waste. Harpur put the kettle on and tried to get his head straight. They sat down at the table. Helen said: 'In the car, I've got your Christmas present from Denise. She thought it best not to send it here. She says she'll come down again some time during the vacation. It's tricky for her, Colin – fearful of intruding on the mourning.'

He nodded and went to make the instant. 'Jack's got problems?'

'For the moment he's all right, but I don't know.'

Harpur sat down again, drank a little coffee, waited and watched her. She was about Denise's age, around twenty, pale, small featured, almost demure looking, somewhere between beautiful and very beautiful. These days, she went in for quite severe, business-style clothes and had on a light blue woollen suit and white silk blouse tonight with thin black cravat. She was as clever as anyone Harpur had ever met, including Denise, and possibly even Iles, and already knew more about some aspects of Jack's picture trade than he did himself. Her special corner was *l'art fang*.

'He's not seeing straight, Col.'

'Jack does things his own way.'

'He thinks he's injured you hellishly. Some tapes? That's as much as he'd say. But he goes on about having to put matters right.'

'What's that mean, for God's sake?'

'I don't know. I hoped you would. He said on no account was I to be in touch with you about this at present. So, here I am.'

'I'm boozed, Helen. I'm not seeing straight either.' He thought he did probably see, though. 'But, no, I don't understand. He played me some confidential tapes, yes. I forced him to.'

'He says he shouldn't have. Had carefully decided he wouldn't, then did.'

'Right. I conned him, provoked him. One of my few skills.'

She stared at Harpur. 'Colin, I know you can lie like a master. Jack's always admired that. But, honestly, you don't know what he might do? I had this feeling as he talked – a feeling of risk? This is physical risk, not just money or deals. Jack doesn't sweat or shake or anything like that when he's scared, but if you know him you can read it. His voice narrows right down, his body goes stooped so his clothes seem to hang? It makes me cry. In private.'

124

As you would expect from Helen, this was exactly Lamb touched by terror. 'No,' Harpur said. 'I've no idea what putting it right means. There's nothing to put right.'

'Like obsessive,' she said. 'These tapes – they did you damage somehow?'

'Oh, some damage. Not Jack's fault. He's only the messenger.'

He watched her again, as she thought about this. Perhaps Lamb really had not told her what they were and what was on them. Perhaps he really had not let her listen: the cum chorus, the menu discussions of each other. They went out to her car to collect the present.

'I'll think about things when my mind's clearer,' he said. 'If he talks of going to London, I'd like to hear. Right away, Helen.'

'You *do* know then? What is there in London, Colin? Please.'

'Right away,' he replied, waving her off.

'So, who is she?' Hazel asked.

'Lovely,' Jill said. 'And who's Jack?'

'And a present, too?' Hazel said.

'Who is she, Dad?' Jill asked.

'To me this looks like something of maximum police confidentiality,' Darren replied.

Chapter 28

Five paces. It would be five. Megan worked this out in advance. Walked, not run. Five paces from the tailgate to the driver's door and when that proved exactly right, without stretching or shortening any pace, she felt radiantly satisfied. It would be fine. Her brain was working a treat. Her eyes were working a treat, gauging distance. She was in control, easily remembering to step over the raised perimeter bricks of the parking spot: you could stumble, brain yourself and come to stretched out alongside your vehicle very cold and corpselike on this imitation gravestone, if you did come to. A December night was wrong for sleeping outdoors. She had the key ready in her hand, and no shaking, and could more or less make out the keyhole, despite super bloody shadows from those venomous trees thickening the darkness on this side. Five paces was only five paces and for most of the little time it took she kept her gaze on where she was going, that door, but she did have a chance, too, for a direct, hard, even brave gaze at and among the disgusting trees, and there was definitely nobody about, cashing in on the treacherous cover.

Yes, vague and buried horror memories from *Hansel and Gretel* and *Babes in the Wood* just had to explain her previous untidy panic. Plus, also maybe, sloppy moral guilt feelings. She must have been unconsciously, stupidly expecting punishment, thought Nature in tree form must turn against her! Weak and deeply farcical.

It amused her to find that for, say, three of those five paces, she was concentrating so ferociously on the car door that its navy panel and rectangle of window took on for a second the impression in her mind of a navy and silver flag, a standard, the hinged pillar its pole. It seemed to inspire. It seemed to float and beckon. That was in part the shifting reflection of the tossed trees, but also she so wanted it to seem floating and free of this spot, she so wanted it to recruit her. The door panel was spattered with mud, but that could happen to a battle flag. Strutting on high heels and holding nothing more warlike than a car key, she saw herself for a moment as like a soldier rallying to the banner. How comic. Yet she did feel revitalized, compared with all those shilly-shallying doubts when she loitered at the tailgate. She knew now she had hit the right option. Well, she knew now there had been no call for other options – the possible stupid dash back to the foot-bridge – the possible abject cowering on the far side of the car – no call because the supposed danger was . . . was only supposed. And supposed in a craven fever. Nobody would have seen her make that daft gallop towards the bridge, but she would still have for ever felt ludicrous and ashamed of herself. Nobody would have seen her mocking up trench war-fare on the far side of the Astra, with the car as protective parapet, but she would still have come to wonder what the hell she was doing, and how long she should go on doing it.

At the door and scratching about momentarily for the key-hole, she thought the noise of the wind-battered trees behind her had now grown almost amiable and consoling. There was a kind of sad rhythm, a soothing fluctuation of loud and soft, a nice heavy insistent rustle of the leaves, and regular mellow creaking of the big protesting branches. And, of course, the thing about most of these fairy tale woods was that they did turn out benign, offering children the very com-fort denied them by humans. Nature was a safe, warm bed, not a bloody ambush.

Chapter 29

In the middle of the room, the ACC suddenly crouched forward, his arm and hand out ahead, shirt agleam, silver cufflinks bright under the strip light. He fiddled for a long moment, as though seeking the Astra keyhole in the dark, concentrating, not looking behind. Then, violently, he jerked straight, his head snapping back, and turned swiftly through 180 degrees so he was facing Harpur in his armchair. You could imagine Iles had been spun around by some force outside himself. His face showed surprise, terror, appalling vulnerability under the grey cowlick.

'There was a bruise on her right shoulder,' he said, 'conceivably a grab mark. Possibly she was gripped hard from behind and manhandled – manhandled up and around to face the attacker, though it could, of course, have been caused during standard sex playfulness in London: as we know, there was evidence of recent intercourse, front apparently only, though not as recent as the car park. If, however, the bruise was made by the attacker, it would suggest either someone who wanted an infallible identification, or was experienced enough to appreciate that a knife in the back is very approximate art.'

Over a space of, say, fifteen seconds, Iles's upper body now gave three big shuddering movements. Then he staggered for a couple of moments before folding to the floor near one of the easel legs supporting a blackboard. He came to rest folded in on himself, exactly as Harpur had found Megan. Looking up from there to the Chief, his hand on the wounds area, Iles said: 'Although these three blows under the ribs did not in fact kill at once, as we're aware, she would never have survived, even if hospitalized immediately. This was a stab expert. Colin did what he could, but—'

'Perhaps we should leave all this now,' Lane said.

Four of them were in the ACC's office: Lane, Iles, Garland and Harpur. At the centre of the room was the old-fashioned blackboard and easel on which a section of the car park had been carefully drawn in white chalk, with Megan's Astra as a rectangle on its spot and done in red, plus the bordering trees crowded together, marked as thirteen numbered green crosses and labelled for species. Her body was in white, a matchstick form hard against the red box, arms and legs splayed, not at all the huddled shape Iles had represented: but this would be artistic licence for the matchstick mode. It made her look even more destroyed, as if flattened by some enormous, carefree force.

On two boards taking all one wall were pinned about thirty colour photographs of the car park and the Astra and trees from all angles, Megan absent, of course: by then, past the care of even that terse girl doctor and under a sheet in the hospital side room, or processed to the morgue. The shots were an early December morning job and the photographer seemed to have over-apertured to counter poor light, so the colours looked bright and bogus, like a breezily restored old oil painting. At least ten photographs did the trees and the bit of muddy ground in front, and another ten were close-ups of the Astra's driver's side. Two more had been taken at the rear of the vehicle and showed the tailgate from left and right. There were two of the footbridge and the rest gave general car park views and had ink compass bearings in purple at their top right-hand corners.

The Chief had rung down to Harpur saying that a meeting on the Megan case was 'sort of springing up, Colin, in the ACC's office', and asked Harpur whether he would like to attend. 'But not to feel obliged,' the Chief went on, in his gentle, tentative way: what Iles called Lane's Welfare Wanker's tone. 'Some matters might be specific and painful and there is no need for you to endure them. I thought simply that to ask you was a courtesy.'

'Thank you, sir,' Harpur had replied. 'I'll come.' His second courtesy invitation: people were fine, considerate. Lane had thought a lot of Megan. Many had thought a lot of her, and rightly. There was a time when Harpur thought a lot of her himself and, in his way, he had to the finish. Yes, in his way. This was marriage. He had taken the lift to Iles's room. Mark Lane liked get-togethers that 'sort of sprang up' rather than formally arranged meetings, and preferably not in his own suite. His style was relaxed, or what Iles termed shagged out.

Iles picked himself up now. Despite the performance, he looking superbly brisk in the handmade shirt, silver tie and dark grey suit trousers. He went to sit sideways in a black leather easy chair beneath the photographs, his legs hanging over one of its arms. 'Obviously, we've talked to everyone of substance who might vendetta Col or his family, sir, and particularly everyone who survives in that slimy Webb dynasty, after Harpur blasted their lad so brilliantly at the Link Street Post Office raid. Nothing. I've sprained both knees trying to kick shit out of the alibis. Defeat, though.'

Crew-cut and alert, Francis Garland was sitting behind Iles's desk in his ginger bomber jacket and said: 'Plus, we've had Carbiddy and Antichrist Jessop and Hector Longville in, but again no luck. I thought possible bile there: Mr Harpur and I gave their people a hard time lately – like the Antichrist's mother went down for threats and receiving. Jessop was affronted, asking would he do anything so low against an officer he held in supreme long-term respectful hate, or his lady?'

'Antichrist's sweet,' Iles explained.

The Chief still wore his black tie, though Harpur himself no longer bothered. Lane, seated straight on a straight chair, said in a weak whisper: 'Sometimes I think this patch is – well, is slipping from our control, Desmond.' He waved an arm wearily towards the blackboard then at the window and all the tainted acres extending outside.

'Never with you there,' Iles replied. He also gestured, though more powerfully – pointing at the ceiling and the Chief's suite above, but as if beyond that, at some overlordship office in the sky.

Sunk too far in worry, the Chief did not seem to notice this reply. 'The Press. These appalling suggestions that Megan might have been victimized as retaliation against Colin by some gang he's targeted. Is this Sicily, then? You see, my fear is that our predicament here is symptomatic of the irrepressible rise of evil throughout the country. Are we finally succumbing to the victorious march of hell?'

Behind the desk, Garland rolled one of his eyes, a trick he had. With what looked like folded laboratory reports, Iles brushed something microscopic from his black lace-ups: 'At your rank, you automatically take the wider view, sir. What Chiefship is about. And, if I may say, it is rightly almost a philosophical stance, yet in no way airy-fairy or impractical. The reverse. You spot these universal trends, sir, but, by the Lord, you know how to fight them. That's the crucial thing. This is leadership. This is preservation of the social fabric. Col, we get mention of a so-far unaccounted-for twenty-fiveish dark-haired man, moustached, fur-collared expensive dark coat, on the train. This is from the guard. Mean much to you? Your friends, damp Rog and juicy Coral, say they didn't see him.'

'Should be findable,' Harpur replied.

'We've done an appeal, of course. He hasn't come forward. So, we're intrigued. Rings no bell?'

'I don't think so,' Harpur replied.

Lane stood, smoothing his sallow cheeks slowly with one hand. He had a brownish suit on that would do for now and a decent striped shirt. He wore no shoes – one of his habits around the building, aimed at the informality he wanted. This morning he sported clean white very short gym socks, with blue and red bands at the top, visible when he was seated. Possibly, Iles's remark about the Chief's grander philosophical role had reached and encouraged him and he asked sadly: 'Consider: even when we used to win, could we win only by cheating? The Birmingham Six, the Guildford Four and so on. Now things like that are exposed, will what was good and strong in policing be swept away with what was corrupt? Who, who will guard the people?' His voice became a croak, a gasping plea for assurance.

'You, sir,' Iles instantly replied. He swung around to sit straight in the chair, as though keen to deal formally with Lane's bulky *angsts*.

The Chief said: 'Desmond, I—'

'You have guarded them, and will, sir. If I were asked to, God forbid, specify an inscription for your gravestone, it would be, "Guardian of the people." '

Lane's face seemed to grow greyer with anguish and despair. 'You're kind, Desmond.'

'I speak only what we all feel, sir.' Iles glanced forcefully at Garland and Harpur.

'Certainly,' Garland said.

'I'm sure of it,' Harpur said.

'And it is gross of me to bring my woolly griefs to a room which already has enough real grief of its own,' Lane replied, waving again towards the blackboard. 'Please, forgive me, Colin.'

Iles said: 'Fish meals recovered from the carriage and traces in her handbag. We've had an analysis and it appears they are of exceptionally high quality – beyond anything you could buy in the multiples. Halibut, lobster, Dover sole, etc. Apparently, there's a top-class food place off Lower Bond Street which does its own frozen stuff, at fifteen quid a nibble. I told them on the phone what the lab says are ingredients and they agree these could be theirs.'

'Fish? But what do we make of that, Desmond?' the Chief asked.

Iles said: 'Bought for some private party in London, forgotten in the excitement of the moment, then ditched because they had thawed?'

'What does that mean, "some private party"? The "excitement of the moment"?' Lane said.

Iles stayed silent.

Stricken, Lane glanced at Harpur. 'Oh, of course, of course, Desmond,' the Chief said.

'We might ask the food shop if they remember a purchaser,' Iles said. He stood up, moved to the blackboard, pointing at a spot between tree seven and eight. 'Francis thinks he stood here. Two beeches.'

'Soft ground,' Garland said, 'and we have what could be prints of a man waiting, size tens, then perhaps pulling back and standing further into the cover. Behind number twelve, a birch. Perhaps he thought he'd been spotted.'

As the Chief had said, Harpur was finding some agony here

today. But he would put up with that. He had been due to sit in as observer on a promotion board, one he was damn pleased to dodge. Erogenous Jones was coming up again for the move to inspector and would again be turned down, despite unbeatable gifts. Harpur revered Erogenous and often needed him. Soon, he might need him more than ever and was happy to be spared this morning from observing his neat, lineless face register instantly again the board's sewn-up response, and was happier still not to be observed by Erogenous observing him. Harpur could never decide if the block on Erogenous was just. The world's greatest tail, and probably second only to Iles as the world's greatest interrogator, Sgt. Jeremy Stanislaus Jones was also physically fearless, mentally nifty, and a scintillating brick-wall when cross-examined by even the foulest QC. But Erogenous could not organize, felt sorry for those who could and did, and did not always work to instructions. Of course, nobody with a brain always did, but when Erogenous didn't it could be large scale. Arguably – and more – one of his variations on orders had caused Harpur to shoot a man dead in the Link Street Post Office ambush, or Erogenous himself might have been shot. People noticed such things, especially as this was not Erogenous's first act of dud originality. He would probably go no further, not even as a late pension-hike device.

Lane shuffled across the room and stood squarely in front of the blackboard, alongside Iles. The Chief put a finger on the Astra and moved it in a slow, wide arc: 'If she had seen him, why didn't she get back around the other side of the car, or even make a dash for the bridge?'

'We've wondered,' Iles replied.

'The car would have been a kind of defensive barrier,' Lane said.

'Megan was not a panicky lady, of course,' Iles replied.

'And she might not have been absolutely sure,' Garland said. 'Possibly he was super cautious. Or she calculated her safest ploy was get in fast, relock and drive off. Perhaps she had her key ready in her hand. We recovered it from the tailgate lock, but that was probably him – when he shifted the stuff out.'

Garland liked holding the floor and had a loud, metallic

133

style, of exposition, and generally: Iles used to say he could get a job as a steel band.

'So, the assumption hardens that this was someone waiting specifically for Megan?' Lane asked. He moved away and took his straight chair again, sitting tense and cagey, like pictures Harpur had seen in the paper of a kid next for confession.

'Possibly. Not necessarily,' Garland replied. 'It certainly appears to have been someone waiting near her car, yes, maybe because the Astra was known, or on account it was comparatively isolated, inviting an attack. It's a small car, a model often used by women – family second vehicle.' Garland was a whizz kid who would whizz far and knew it, and meant others to know it. He must enjoy speaking from behind Iles's big, cluttered desk, and enjoy the view of himself in the ACC's full-length wall mirror, fixed so Iles could check the beauty of his uniform on ceremonial days. Harpur realized there were in fact four whizz kids in this room, none old, all well on in rank for age, but probably only Francis convinced he would go further. It was a bonny frame of mind and Harpur hoped it could last. If only Erogenous had a bit of Garland's mental tidiness, and ability to bend the system all ways while play-acting deference to it.

'Someone stalking a woman, but to what purpose, Francis?' Lane asked. 'No sexual motive, no theft.'

'Possibly interrupted,' Iles replied.

'But we've had nobody come forward and say they saw her or him?' Lane asked.

'People don't always come forward, sir,' Garland stated. 'Especially people out very late for their own reasons.'

Of course, Lane did not have to be told that. He had once been a polished rough-house detective and knew how things were. But in this top job he would pretend now and then to a kind of innocence: his way of asserting that sound old values did still exist and that the norms in life were decent norms and could be taken for granted. This might be part of his philosophical stance, too: a sort of fingers-crossed philosophy which would not have fooled Bertrand Russell. High office brought them right down. Think of Lucifer.

The Chief said: 'How does all this fit in with your fur-collared man? He's on the train, but also ahead of her, waiting?'

'He might have deliberately hurried,' Garland replied. 'And she's loaded with four carrier bags. It's possible she went to the lavatory.'

'Did he get on at London?' Lane asked.

'The guard thinks so,' Garland said.

'Yet knows her car?'

'Not impossible, sir. If people have been keeping an eye on her for a chance. On Mr Harpur's family generally,' Garland said.

'Doing *what*, for God's sake?' Lane replied. 'A chance? Which people?'

'Find the fur collar and we might know, sir,' Iles said. 'The guard tells us he seemed to contemplate getting out at Dobecross, or maybe pretended to. This was when he became noticeable. Now, as to the assault, we think she was totally surprised. It would seem she believed all was well, perhaps had managed to convince herself, con herself. Possibly attacked while still bending to unlock the door. Her arms were uninjured, so we must assume she had no time to resist or attempt self-protection.' Iles turned to Harpur. 'No private tips your way, Col? This offence would disgust all sorts, not just Antichrist. I wondered if some of those wonderful friends had intimated in your pretty ear.'

'They'd know for sure I wouldn't be handling it, sir.'

Moving fast, Iles came and stood over the armchair and snarled down: 'OK, don't answer. Even in your sorrow you fuck me about, Harpur, hoard your stinking privacies? You've heard voices?'

'Please, Desmond,' Lane said.

'If this is London-originated, none of my local informants would have sources,' Harpur told Iles. 'Surely.'

'Surely, Desmond,' Lane said.

Cutting off Garland's view of the mirror, the ACC went to brush his trousers down and gaze at himself in it for a good while. His cowlick had lurched during the death act and with the back of his hand he pushed it higher on his brow. As essential to his role just now, he had managed to seem female and helpless. Now, Iles was back to himself: very compact, male, lean, cuckoldable, jaunty.

'How I hate to hear policing reduced to this – whispers, voices,' the Chief declared. 'Such sick dependency on undesirables.'

Without turning, and smiling to himself very fondly in the glass, Iles replied: 'Not all policing, obviously, sir. Not traffic direction or lost dogs. Harpur's wife might be, though, a different kettle of, as it were, fish.'

Harpur hung on in the ACC's room when the Chief and Garland left. 'Christmas, sir,' he said.

'Both of us truly look forward to welcoming the three of you, Col, at our modest but sincere homage to this joyous festival. And so does Fanny. The age-old glistening holy story – always so restorative.' He hummed and half sang with godly relish the opening of 'As With Gladness'. 'I don't know about asking Garland and whatever fanny with a small f he's got in tow just now. That business he had with Sarah. But, then, you, too. Then again, perhaps she was in need. These things come and go, don't they? All of us are certainly under a rigid obligation to bear grudges in life, though at a deeper level than Christmas parties. Yet I wouldn't sabotage Francis's career prospects, not at all, nor yours, if you had any, Harpur.'

'Thank you very much, sir. I knew that.'

'One wants vengeance, yes, but vengeance with tone.'

'This boyfriend of Hazel – a problem, sir. His mother's rather negative, unfulsome, even anti-police.'

'As the Chief says, all very reasonable and widespread. Difficult to rebut. Well, you know this – your kids' attitude to us.'

'If the boy isn't able to come, I don't think Hazel will. She says she'll drop him, but I can't believe it. And I could hardly leave her on Christmas Day, not the first without Megan. We'd all have to give your place a miss, I'm afraid.'

Something like collapse took his smooth, bone-strong face. 'Oh, God, Col, this is disastrous,' Iles replied.

'What? You mean Hazel not showing? Or all of us? Hazel's still only a child, you know, sir.'

'We can surely put this right, somehow, can't we? I say

136

again, this is the apogee of the Christian year, Col. We need you and yours there.'

'I wondered if you'd call on the mother, have a word. I think you could influence her, sir. You would speak so well of the thin blue line and our right to, and profound need of, public support against the mounting evil as cited by the Chief. The husband's away from the house all day on a normal nine to five office job. She's not aged, or sickly. No, lively in a combative way, which can be stimulating. I feel she would be very responsive to well-honed argument.'

'Well, I could take a look at that. I hate to hear of a lad persecuted, and he's not grossly possessive, or anything like that, is he? Harpur, you'll obviously want to know my real view of the fish. Not exactly what I said to Lane, of course. Col, Col, it's tragic, but the Chief's so delicate and requires continuous shielding. I see this as the main part of my duties, the lovely, genial, confused cunt. She and Tambo go to some provided flat which is nicely stocked for them on the famous quid pro quo basis. Megan can swallow the flat and probably so on, but not the freezer meals. Last strawism. Tambo's afraid of offending the cornucopia, whoever, so they take the packets to dispose of.'

'What flat, sir? You said Tambo told you they went out to Highbury.'

'Yes, he did. These meals are not Highbury.' Iles was at his desk now and lowered his shining grey head for a bit of a gaze at the top, significantly. 'Col, Tambo looked to me, sounded to me, like an all-round sell-out. In someone's pocket for gain? Forgive me, I really hate saying this about a man your wife so conscientiously day-tripped to screw, but it's so. That extra strong jaw-line and super-steady eyes they work for when doing the dubious? Like one of those TV evangelists or Jimmy Thomas.'

'Who?'

'Don't you know *anything*, Harpur? Labour Minister. A financial scandal.'

'Oh, *that* Jimmy Thomas. 1936. He could do a strong jaw-line? Podgy faced, wasn't he? So, where's the gifted flat, sir? Any real backing for this idea?'

'I'm still at the sniffing stage, Col. She never said anything herself about the address? District would help. But is she likely to, for God's sake, I ask? Even in the most token marriage like yours a wife would not discuss the nature of away-play venues. Proprieties I love, don't you, Harpur, especially when everything around is dropping from rot?

Chapter 30

Her first London outing to meet Tambo had been a huge adventure, needing such planning, such tact, such cheek. She was not sure whether Colin saw why she wanted to go, but for propriety's sake, and for the sake of harmony at home, she must present an acceptable case. Some delicacy, some consideration for his feelings and pride were essential. This was basic politeness. Neither of them would want to hurt the other unnecessarily.

On the train she experienced two anxieties. First, although she would be away for only a day, it seemed like desertion, particularly of the children. In fact, the children had encouraged her to go, but groaned over the culture calls she planned. In their ad jargon they said she deserved an away-break, if seeing *The* cowing *Way of the World* was that. She had always genuinely loved London, and suggesting this trip for herself could hardly shock Colin or the girls, but she felt nervy proposing it so soon after Tambo moved there. Of course she did: she knew the intent, and guilt clung to her for most of the journey. Crazy, crazy, crazy: should she check in the lavatory mirror she had not changed into a scarlet woman!

Her other anxiety was slighter. Tambo's divorce had gone through and he lived alone. He had taken a small place somewhere out between Islington and Highbury, and she did not find this too thrilling. It knocked the adventure aspect of the trip, made it seem seedy. By that, she did not mean for a moment that these districts were seedy, nor the people who lived in them. Brought up by parents of wide and tolerant outlook, she hoped she could never drop into such class crudity. And, in fact, a central feature of London's charm was that all sorts lived everywhere, giving variety and an exciting social mix. Simply, though, the area he had picked was not what she visualized when she thought London. She was sensitive to place. This discrimination, also, she had picked up from her parents, who quite possessively revelled in some spots – parts of Paris, parts of Seville, parts of Edinburgh – and were sharply offended by other spots – parts of Paris, parts of Seville, parts of Edinburgh.

Obviously, London could not be all West End and Belgravia, and these super-rich regions failed to enrapture her, anyway. The kind of districts Megan really felt at ease in and appreciated were, say, the busy but characterful St John's Wood, or Highgate, of course, where she was brought up, or – another of course – Hampstead, where she had a Fabian Society uncle and aunt, and where so many interesting folk lived, and the book shops kept admirably up to date with post-colonial novels. She feared it would seem demoralizing to trek out to some banal street in Highbury – so like Highgate in spelling, so different in flavour – to trek out there for their first love-making since Tambo came to this job. Naturally, she knew Islington had become reasonably in, but the borders of that and Highbury sounded a drab no man's land – say like the region between Hampstead and Golders Green, though poorer – and this would be true no matter how pleasant his flat might be. Unsmart. If this was a snobbish verdict, too bad.

The point was, she loved to think of Tambo in the big London setting, and as someone important in it. To see him cornered in a workaday area would be all wrong, especially on their reunion. Perhaps later it might be less damaging. She wondered if this said something about the affair. Did Tambo need to be glamorized for her? Was what she felt for him shallow? This troubled Megan. She could imagine her parents' view: although they would be understanding and wholly adult about infidelity when it was a serious, perhaps irresistible, relationship, they would feel hurt terribly by anything at all shoddy and meaningless. It was what they would term in others 'mere self-indulgence'. But perhaps when you reached your mid thirties, everyone needed glamorizing. She would not mind some for herself, and worked at it with the brush and tweezers, spent on it.

And then, when she had met Tambo at the station, he said at once that there could be no question of trekking out to what he called his 'dreary pad in dreary Highbury'. He had booked a room at a decent, small hotel in South Kensington. She almost threw her arms around his neck and kissed him right there on the station – she felt such delight that his mind operated in harmony with hers. In particular she exulted at his choice of that word 'trekking', the very one which had come into her own head.

However, she restrained her happiness and did not touch him quite yet, simply filled her eyes with him. There was time for kissing and its accompaniment in the hotel very soon afterwards, and it could not have been a more pleasant road, nor a nicer hotel. It was early spring then, and the sun glinted on brass door fittings, on new paint and clean windows. Tambo had taste. He, too, was sensitive to place. This instinctive rapport convinced her absolutely that, no, there was nothing superficial or cheap about their relationship, nothing shallow. They understood each other effortlessly, were marvellously alike and suited. Her parents might well come to like him, although more fuzz. Megan's relief broke out in wonderful, violent, yet tender love-making, a telling reassertion of things after separation. She was sure it would never have been like this in Islington/Highbury and felt no squeamishness at such a thought, because he had realized it, too. Sucking and being sucked in such a setting would have been mere engaging routines from *How To Brighten Your Sex Life*, but here they were grand items in a glorious pattern of avowals. 'You taste like the future and it works,' she mumbled.

Although it was only a few weeks since he came up to the new job, she felt she saw in him already additional poise and resolve. That thrilled her. It would be absurd to slight this new assurance by regarding it only as glamour. She could tell just by gazing at him in that first moment on the station that Tambo was strong enough and talented enough to, as it were, capitalize on what the capital offered. His features had always been resolute – firm chin, unflinching eyes, good nose: hence, in part, Tamburlaine, though it was not all looks, and he had real acting flair. Obviously, not even London could work a facial change in weeks, but he seemed to relay even more fine solidity and confidence. The big challenges here brought people on, stretched them, developed them fast, as long as they could take the pace and pressure, and she was sure Tambo could. Well, didn't she see he could? Would she have picked a man who could not?

'How's my successor?' he had asked.

'Iles? Not seen much of him. Dangerous? Violent? Unstoppable? Yes, unstoppable. He thinks the police can win.'

'Some of us do.'

'I think it hurts him to deal with those who don't. The Chief. Iles seems liable to hit out with terrible legal-or-not ferocity. And then his wife. She seems to be looking for it. Is the hotel a terrible expense, Tambo?'

'It's not very often, Megan, unfortunately.'

'I'd really like it if we could always come here.'

'Yes,' he said. 'Our place.'

'Is this unreasonable? Superstitious, almost?'

'Darling, of course not. It's just our kind of spot.'

Chapter 31

Harpur decided he ought to look at this nest address in May-fair. It was the only geography he had, except for Hazel's list of the shops, and she and Iles had already toured those. If Tambo hid this place from Iles, it was special. That is, if Iles had not lied about what Tambo told him. Iles could be as professional as anyone, and more.

The children would be fine. He announced he might have a couple of days in town to do his own Christmas shopping and asked if there was anything they wanted. 'The Chief says I should take it easy for a while after the shock.'

'Now you're going sniffing, too, are you, Dad?' Jill asked. 'A vengeance mission?'

'So what do we tell Iles if he calls?' Hazel said.

'I'm visiting Mum's parents, to sort out her papers. She's intestate.'

'He'll believe that?' Hazel asked.

'Sort out her affairs?' Jill asked.

'That's it.'

'Dad, you've got some extra facts about the paramour?' Jill said.

'Iles will have a word with Scott's mother,' Harpur replied.

'I thought he liked them younger,' Hazel said. 'I *know* he likes them younger.'

'Siren,' Jill replied.

Harpur said: 'I'll tell Francis Garland I'm going. He'll keep an eye here. The slightest bother, give him a ring, or if he's not around, 999 as a last resort.'

'Or Erogenous?' Jill said. 'I like Erogenous.'

'I know he's away on a case,' Harpur replied. Erogenous he needed.

'Pull the curtains over?' Jill asked.

'No need to go mad,' Hazel replied. 'That woman's not crushing me. Dad, you're really interested enough to follow Mum's tracks?' Hazel said.

'Don't be so damned casual,' Jill told her. 'After all, this was his wife.'

'Yes, after all,' Hazel said.

It puzzled Harpur, too. Of course, he was a cop, and if cops had a speck of special knowledge, they used it. The address was a speck. He would look at the voters' register for the company's name, and then he might have two specks. But he knew there was more to it than police automatic response. He felt he owed her a bit: more than he would owe any other victim. Well, certainly, certainly. As Jill said, after all, this was his wife. He found he had a growing rage against Tambo, not so much for taking her from him as for landing Megan in something and then not looking after her. Was there a touch of the voyeur, wanting to ogle the venue? You've heard the roars now see the stadium. But it would be the venue that pulled her into danger, so perhaps curiosity was all right.

'What additional stuff, anyway, Dad?' Jill asked. 'It points somewhere? Obviously, you know the lover. Singular? And so does Iles. How did you get it if you're supposed to be sunk in mourning?' Her voice cracked.

'He mourns, but in his own style, Jill. How they both are, were. Don't hurt yourself about it. Don't hurt him about it.'

The phone rang and she answered, then handed it to Harpur. 'Non-fink. A woman. Girl? Not Helen.'

Denise said: 'OK calling now, once in a while? Your daughter sounds protective. Quite right: you need it. I'm thinking of coming down for a couple more days pre-Yule. Did you open the present?'

'Not yet.'

'Good boy. Wait till Father Christmas says OK.'

'I have to go to London.'

'Why? About Megan? Yes, about Megan.'

'A couple of days.'

'A night? Great. I'll come. Book an hotel. Cut rates – they can't fill them. Say a time and place, Col.'

'How?'

'I'll give them a tale here. Accommodation rang to say I might have to switch flats next term, so I want to examine. Sleep in the bed. I'll come to London instead. Sleep in yours. Nelson's Column?'

'Thanks. Wednesday, 4 p.m.'

She was quiet for a while. Then she said: 'Now I've browbeaten you, I ask, is this really all right, Col? You can tell me sod off if you want to be private. A her and you matter. I'd work at understanding.'

'It's fine.'

'I can't bear to imagine you there alone, that bloody, big, indifferent tip of a place, thinking about your wife and taking a beating from memories and regrets. Is this presumptuous? But, then, I am. Col, do you think you need me?'

'Oh, indeed,' Harpur replied.

'Oh, indeed,' Hazel said, when he put the phone down. 'That's chat-up language?'

'Well, it might be an idea to pull the curtains as far as they'll go,' Harpur replied.

Chapter 32

It had been on her fifth London trip that she first heard about, went to, Careen Street. She had had a giggle on the train about all those earlier frets. This was going to be a superb day: the Raphael exhibition that everyone loved, and then *Volpone*. She had been stupid and a bit egomaniac to fear the children would feel ditched. They accepted her outings now, knew she would be back when they woke up in the morning: knew also she would be back with presents and interesting tales of the big city. They did not want a housebound mother. They knew people were entitled to a life.

It was early autumn, and Tambo had on a foul mauve sweatshirt, which she praised thoroughly as soon as they met at the station. 'Such a piece of luck, Meg,' he said. 'I've been offered use of an apartment. Mayfair.'

'But that's very select.'

'A friend. He says drink the champagne, what's more.'

'Which friend is that, Tambo?'

'He runs a few businesses. I bumped into him through the job. He's absolutely OK. No strings.'

'So farewell our hotel? I feel quite sad. It's stupid.'

'But we'll see it again, probably. I don't suppose the flat will be eternally available.'

'Who else uses it?'

'A company facility.'

There was still about Tambo that new, strong, London poise which she liked so much, found so sexy, if it had to be spelled out. On top of that today and recently, she thought she felt something else. It was tricky to say what, but the word that kept nudging her was – money. This was not just better wages, which would have come with his move here and promotion. This was – well, money. Her mother always used to say you could smell it on those who had it, and perhaps she did not mean that well. Her parents approved of and had a good earned income. The presence of something over and above made them uneasy, jabbed their tender politics. What Tambo seemed to radiate lately was something over and above. Megan did not have much politics, but she felt uneasy, and more uneasy when she saw Careen Street and the Taittinger.

'I've had some photographs done,' Tambo said. 'Vanity.'

He spread them alongside their champagne flutes. He had been wearing the sodding sweatshirt when they were taken. 'I must have a couple, Tambo.'

'Why I had them done. Now sit there and choose, while I get you a meal from the freezer.'

'Good Lord, complimentary nosh as well?'

'But not your run-of-the-mill convenience packets. These are gourmet items.'

'Someone thinks a lot of you.'

'Standard provisions here.'

'How did they know you needed the flat, Tambo?'

He had found a chef's blue striped apron in a cupboard and was putting it on. 'Please, I don't talk about us, believe me, Meg. The offer was just put – should I ever need it feel free, you know?' It was this kind of statement, and how Tambo made it, that seemed to say money: all so casual, all as if he were obviously entitled, and obviously belonged.

'And you replied, "Funny you should say that," ' Megan replied.

Silly, minor things seemed to signal a new expansiveness in him. No gold watch or mohair suit, but the sweatshirt, the photographs. Yes, photographs: it was as though Tambo had only lately picked his identity, and she had the idea new funds helped. Did police pose for portraits? Colin went about destroying pictures of himself and reckoned no likeness of Iles as an adult existed outside his dossier and passport.

'It would be a waste not to accept the place, don't you

think, Meg? Almost churlish.' And then, perhaps realizing how smug and grand he might have sounded he said: 'It's childish and vulgar, I suppose, but I like being seen going in and out of a place like this.'

'Depends who by.'

Chapter 33

On the train to London, Harpur tried to tell Erogenous how things were without telling him: without exactly saying that, in his case, promotion boards were for ever fixed, and why ask them to piss on you every two years? Impossible to know if Erogenous read the message. He stayed as cheerful as ever, his features somewhere between friendly and blank, the face of a fine interrogator. Talking to someone hunting a job was like talking to a lover: they would seem to follow the conversation, whatever it was – Sarajevo, veal and ham pies, the royals – but you knew that all the time they were picking at your words, looking for the only things that interested them, looking for their destiny and nobody and nothing else's. The lover wanted to know, do you still fancy me, have you been with someone else, what do you think of my hair-do, slim-down, tooth-cap? The promotion hope wanted to know, is it for me this time, please God, and are you doing all you can, you bastard, and above?

Harpur needed him for this outing to Mayfair. If it came to tailing, he had to have the best. This was a foreign realm and there must be no errors. Iles had not much use for Erogenous's special flairs on the Megan inquiries, and his absence from the patch could be covered: Harpur would fake a couple of days' work sheets as for other cases, and they did his fare, accommodation and subsistence through the tipster fund, where accounting was so beautifully vague.

But that one worry had dogged Harpur from the start. Erogenous would see the trip as an extra, off-the-record gift to Harpur. It called for a return: influence with the promotion people. Erogenous was a grand lad, not grasping beyond the norm, but he had a long-service medal and knew how police forces ran – on influence: on nods, winks, hates, handshakes, on unpublished and unpublishable debts of gratitude, on quietly owing and being owed. Erogenous would assume that if the detective chief superintendent wanted a sergeant to move up he would move up, and historical black marks could be Copydexed. So, get the chief super indebted: agree to travel unofficially with him on what looked like a private hit-back mission.

There was something in all this, but not enough. Harpur remained unsure Erogenous could handle higher rank. Tails tailed. Leaders lead. Plus, successive people higher than Harpur had noted Erogenous's fuck-you-colonel-sir way with orders. Iles considered Erogenous almost wrecked Link Street. And if the ACC had you marked low you languished. It was tough telling someone this when he was doing you a favour, but Harpur felt he had to try.

Chapter 34

Autumn. This would have been Trip Seven, probably, and she had felt absolutely all right. A routine, now? A routine with its lovely opportunities and its understood limits? Perhaps Tambo did not understand them in the way she did. But love affairs could be like that.

From the train window the countryside looked rich and serene. She would have felt absolutely all right if the countryside had been scruffy and poor: she did not believe in Nature as mood maker or destroyer. Simply, a decent outlook was a plus.

It was going to be an Impressionists exhibition this time, a school she adored – perhaps even more than she esteemed Raphael, though that show had been as magnificent as all the notices said. There had been raves for 'The Impressionists', too: 'rarely can so many works of such quality have been gathered in one gallery' – that kind of irresistible gush. A few critics had particularly gone to town on the Manets. She thought most highly of him among the Impressionists, so all in all this exhibition could not be more up her street. She rhapsodized over it last night to the children, who did their usual philistine stuff, well learned from Colin. Of course, when Colin did his philistine bit they heckled him for that.

'They really get people in to look at this stuff?' Hazel said.

'It will be crowded. I'll have to queue, I expect.'

'Don't you feel . . . well, lonely up there?' Jill asked. 'Crowds, and by yourself.'

'Too much to do, too many places to get to. Then *The Homecoming*.'

'Is that the last train or a play?' Hazel asked.

By now, Megan had almost grown used to the flat in Careen Street, and had almost forgotten the nice little South Kensington hotel. Tambo would be hurt if she went on quibbling, and why give distress? He did not deserve that. She wanted to take back the thought that he had been transformed by a rush of mystery wealth. He was still Tambo as she had always known him, and as she had come to love him. She could not recall or imagine now what had made her think he was suddenly sitting on extra. The sweatshirt? The photographs? How daft to base a theory on these. He had stopped wearing the sweatshirt, thank God, though she was sure she had always been polite about it.

But, no, of course, he was not quite the same Tambo who worked with Colin. That London assurance and polish were present now. This was the only change, though. She had maligned him. She was coming to realize something which, perhaps, she thought she might have realized and acknowledged years ago: that policing was like no other job, its ethics not easily understood by those outside. Cops lived under the pressure of the streets and their ethics were street ethics. Law they left to lawyers. Gazing at the warm villages and sedate fields, she decided it was as crazy and dismally unjust to blame Tambo for the flat as for the sweatshirt and Happy Snaps.

Chapter 35

Harpur went to see 26 Careen Street. Erogenous would watch it and tail anything tailable, in a couple of proper duty spells. Harpur simply required a quick look from outside. The force of this need had shaken him. Posthumously, on tape, Megan could get to him more than she had done in life for years. Pass the Ouija-board. The recorded yells, those crackling cries of fulfilment, genuine or diplomatic, had come to sound in his memory like cries for help or vengeance. If he had told Denise this he knew she would have called him Hamlet, so he didn't.

He did take her to see 26A. It might seem mad, but he wanted her in on his agonies, even this one. And, with her brassy self-centredness, she might help snuff them out. How much he *would* tell her, he did not know yet. She was bright, demanding and a hurtable child. Erogenous would spot the two of them on the sight-seeing, of course. It did not matter much now, Harpur being single. On the other hand, Harpur would probably not spot Erogenous.

As a tailing job, it was tough. Flat A had its own front door on to the fine street, so anyone who came and went there was eligible. If somebody inside rang for a taxi or had a car, would Erogenous get a cab in time to follow? If he picked one target to go with, would somebody else more useful come out or go in while he was away? 'More useful' here could mean only one thing: they wanted the fur-collar man, preferably still wearing it, but at least with the age and looks. Harpur's instructions to Erogenous were to wait to see if he showed and to log everyone else who visited or left. But with Erogenous, you were never certain he listened and whether he would do it, anyway. Genius took its own route, and occasionally fucked

153

up, in lights. Then, if they located him, where next? Point Iles that way? Deal with it personally? That meant what? Harpur did not formulate and could not. No, he was not Hamlet.

'What is this?' Denise asked.

Harpur, looking at the porticoed door and the big curtained windows, said: 'We've got observation on it.'

'But London. You're allowed?'

'It's special to us.'

She gazed at the flat and then at him. 'Special to *you*?'

'We're in the Regent Palace hotel.'

'Where else?'

'There's a colleague with me, but I've put him on a different floor. Breakfast in the rooms. You won't have to meet.'

'Special to *you*? You're dodging? Can we try for *From a Jack to a King*?'

'Anything. What is it?'

'A show. The *Macbeth* story, but in the rock world.'

'What else?'

'The music's sixties, though, so straight to your withered soul, Col. You know *Macbeth*?'

Perhaps it would be a Shakespeare day. 'Where she falls in love with a donkey?' he replied.

'All right. This is some street. She knew someone in a street like this? How did she get to know someone in a street like this? She came from a great family? Do great families call girls Megan? Lloyd George did, but before he got great, and he was Welsh, so it's forgivable. Christ, am I out of my class, Col – from an executive estate in Stafford? You two moved in this world? I mean, the quality of the railings, so tall and thick. She was fond of this sort of thing?'

'She loathed it.'

'Don't sound so bloody proud of her. I'm glad you brought me. Private grief's a poison.'

'I've heard that. Denise, love, be noisy when we fuck.'

'Here? Aren't I always?'

'Not always.'

'Anyway, why?'

'You will?'

'And you?'

'Oh, yes,' he said.

They walked up towards Bond Street. He had not seen Erogenous, nor anyone in a fur collar, nor anyone who looked as if he or she might hire and brief a fur collar and instruct him to go carefully through all her stuff while she was dying in case something might lead to 26A Careen Street.

'Some sort of vengeance thing, Col – to do with this address?'

'I'm police. Police don't hold with vengeance. You must know that. There's the law.'

'God bless it. Not for everything.'

'Yes. I'd like to buy you your Christmas present while we're here.'

'In Bond Street? Give yourself a chance. This area can go to your head, make you act up. For me, you don't have to keep pace with your wife's friend, friends, whoever. She yelled during?'

'I don't want just yells. Words, Denise, love. Clear words.'

'She did that in there during? It upsets you? How do you know she did?' After a pause, she spoke more quietly. 'But she always did, so you *would* know? You're letting your imagination loose in tribute?' She pushed her face against the arm of his coat as they walked and what she said was now not just half-voice but blurred by herringbone. 'Col, I'm having to cope with a lot of bloody painful information today.'

'Yes, I know.'

'But I can,' she said, 'despite youth.'

'Yes, I know. Anyway, nothing drabber than a silent screw, is there?'

'No screw?' she replied.

Chapter 36

The trip home with Erogenous was not cheerful. In two days he had seen nobody. Perhaps in the run-up to Christmas there were no takers for the flat, business contacts and lovers at home with the family. Erogenous remained his usual chirpy, unreadable self, but he would be disappointed. There had been no chance for brilliance, no chance to stretch Harpur's obligations.

'I went inside,' Erogenous said.

'Inside 26?'

'Inside 26A.'

'Christ, it's bugged.'

'This to do with why we were there? How do you know? I thought probably. I was shoeless, of course, and did without Radio 1. Not visual bugged, though. Obviously, I looked for eyes. Everything beautifully spruce – I'd say professional cleaners.'

'Went inside how? There's broken glass?'

'Oh, would I, Colin? Two locks and good ones but I had plenty of time to work. A surprisingly ancient alarm. If we come again, it's a formality. I'll take you in. Perhaps it's sensitive, though.'

'No, I don't think I'm coming back.'

'The girl can't make it any more? Sweet, brainy-looking kid, and very fond? If I may say. It's a comfort to be with someone like that in an alien land. All round you indifference, but devotion where it matters. Did I recognize her? The Panda? I interested myself. Taittinger in the fridge and grub in the freezer – might be similar to our find? What would that connection be, then, sir? Half a gross of various brand condoms in a bedside cupboard. If I had some idea what it was all about, I'd be clear what to look for. I assume your wife. In what respect, though? It's too grim to talk about, I expect, Colin, and sorry to have pushed it. All the gear top grade, including cutlery. Silk on the beds. Nothing personal anywhere. No clothes, no papers, though a nice repro desk. Named to a company in the list?'

'Yes.'

'We start hunting the directors?'

'I might hand it all over to the ACC,' Harpur said. 'I'm sitting on a lot of stuff. It's wrong, unprofessional, I could come very unstuck.'

Erogenous nodded a few times pretty wisely. 'Of course it's wrong, sir. But you really want to do that? Colin Harpur doesn't come unstuck, or never has, though unconventional now and then. Sitting on a lot of stuff? Maybe. Is it enough? We go home with nothing, except a tour of the town house and kitchen inventory. You're the boss, though.'

'Iles is.'

Erogenous gave what might have been called a sigh in someone else. 'I can't worry much about Mr Iles. He blocks me. Link Street? All right, yes, I went a bit wild. You'd think he shot the boy, not you – for which, thanks. Eternally.'

'How do you know he blocks you?'

'I'm a detective.'

'Iles is fair.'

'Of course he's fair, sir. I don't deserve to go up. Impetuous and ageing – hell of a combination, which doesn't appear in any of the ideal leadership profiles. But police promotion is about who deserves? Since when? Look, people jump ahead of Iles into Chief chairs. I don't think he'd say they deserve it. They just get it. So why can't Erogenous find a low-level bit of late-life favour – put icing on the long-service gong?'

Chapter 37

Trip Eight, mid-November. Next time, she would have to do some Christmas shopping. Not today. She had spent almost the whole journey up trying to recall faces at that Impressionist exhibition last time. This was not faces on canvas, but real faces, crowd faces, the culture and tourist mob, and perhaps somebody extra, perhaps more than one. Naturally, it was hopeless and idiotic, although she had worked at it ever since, not just today. The three rooms of the gallery had been heaving. You battled to get in front of whichever work you wanted to see and had no time to note the looks or clothes or physiques of the people in your way. They were the enemy, to be sidled around or discreetly elbowed or muttered about if they were big and immovable. It was the stuff on the walls you wanted to remember.

All the same, she repeatedly tried to persuade, frog-march, trick her mind into reproducing the moment when Tambo came to her, suddenly looking like prey, and said they had to leave. She wanted details – the features again of people near him, behind him and those further off, too: she could not be sure where he had seen whatever it was he had seen. And the harder she worked at hindsight, and the more she called for pictures not of pictures but of spectators, the more Manet's *The Suicide* monopolized her recollections: the brilliant inertness, the stain, the white of the shirt. Or was the white the bed clothes? God, memory: what a dim power. But the pistol had been in the right hand, hanging from the bed, hadn't it? Surely she had that right, at least. So what? Did this help her find what had shit-scared Tambo?

It was autumn moving fast into winter, and a day of sweeping rain. From the train window, the countryside looked what it was, mud with grass on. But she would not let this depress her. Pretty or drab, it was immaterial. This was still a freedom ride, a love jaunt and a mind mission: they would see *Endgame* today, that frightening parable, with people in dustbins. Yes, Christmas chores on the next outing. This time, though, she wanted to concentrate on Tambo. Some re-affirmation seemed crucial.

When she arrived, she had watched him for traces of that sudden distress and fright in the Impressionists. But, of course, he would be expecting this and blitzed her with normality and joy, his face as lively as an excited child's and stronger than a sea wall. It was good of him to try to console her. It was wonderful he had managed to crawl out of that pit of terror, wonderful even if it had taken him the full three weeks, and she had no evidence of that.

Chapter 38

During school holidays before Christmas, Harpur thought he should try to get home more often now to be with the children. He knew they probably found it a pain, but he went when he could, anyway. Four days before Christmas the telephone rang in the house while he was having a lunchtime line-by-line discussion on the Church of England marriage service with Hazel, Jill and Scott. Erogenous began talking as soon as Harpur picked up the receiver. He did not sound too good. Harpur switched the machine to record.

'I need to know, in case I'm panicking,' Erogenous said.

'What?'

'Panicking.'

'I didn't get the first bit,' Harpur replied.

'Some lad, about twenty-five, dark hair, dark moustache, say twelve stone, six feet.'

'Where is he?' Harpur said.

'You know him? Is he rough and tumble? Do I fret?'

'Where are you?' Harpur replied.

'I think he's behind me. *Me* being tailed!'

'Where are you?'

'A booth. Piccadilly Circus. I came back for another look at 26A. It was hopeless last time. I felt I'd failed you.'

Jesus. 'They were watching for you? Saw the locks had been done, heard the fridge door on tape.'

'I don't leave lock marks. If he's by himself, OK. I can lose him. Perhaps. But I think more than one. Do you know him, Colin? Is this the unknown Iles places on the train? Unknown to Iles. To you, different, as almost always? Could be a paid hunter? No fur collar today, but the rest's right. He moves bloody well.'

'Yes, probably more than one. They'd have a team ready. Dial 999.'

'Well, I might.' His voice trailed off for a moment. 'I'm looking. I don't see him, them, now, but yes, I might. Would I look soft, crying help from the Met for bugger all, sir, or even for something? Shouldn't I handle what I started, and on others' soil? They'd hear about it on the patch. Iles isn't going to be impressed, nor the promotion board. You people at the top prize cool. And would it tangle things for you?'

'Do it,' Harpur said.

Suddenly, he went weighty: 'Colin, if things turn bad, tell Jane I would have made it to inspector, yes? I mean, regardless. It's become crucial to the daft bitch – a mark of my quality as a man, or not.'

'You're at a phone in the Underground station?' Harpur replied.

'Don't you ring them. Col, I might be able to turn this one, get behind him myself. We'd build some knowledge of their crew then. That would be useful to you, yes? This would put things right for Megan. Is he the boy we want?'

'No, I've never heard of him. Sounds like a Mexican embassy clerk.'

'So, why so worried?'

'Give me the booth number,' Harpur replied. Erogenous put the phone down.

Jill said: 'You look terrible.'

'Someone taking stupid risks for a job.'

'Erogenous?' Jill asked. 'He does danger, doesn't he?'

'My mother says that's all police work is, just wanton risk and being shunned,' Scott replied. 'Or she did. Mr Iles called a couple of times at the house and must have given her something to think about.'

'I wouldn't be surprised,' Jill said.

'Erogenous, Dad?' Hazel asked.

'Possibly laying on some drama to make his number with me. He did his own sob RIP then turned cocky as ever.'

'I love Erogenous,' Jill said. 'He doesn't give a monkey's.'

'To do with Mum?' Hazel asked.

'Can you help him?' Jill said.

'Yes,' Harpur replied. He dialled Scotland Yard and gave

them an anon that a man was in danger of his life at Piccadilly station.

'They'll turn out on something so vague? Why are you no-
naming?' Jill asked. 'Wouldn't a cop as cop carry more
weight?'

Scott said: 'There are things under the surface which at our
age we've no clue of.'

'Oh, God,' Hazel replied.

'Is Erogenous married?' Jill asked.

'A long-time live-in.'

'Should she be told?'

'I haven't got anything to tell her,' Harpur said.

'Let's hope it stays like that,' Hazel replied.

'So what fridge?' Jill said. 'What tape? He's been inside
some place for you? Actually inside at hazard?'

'It's to do with Mummy? On tape?' Hazel asked.

'Don't you owe him more than a take-it-or-leave-it call, for
Heaven's sake?'

Scott said: 'There could be policy matters involved here.'

'Yes, I do,' Harpur replied.

He went upstairs and on the bedroom phone dialled Scotland
Yard again. This time he asked for Tambo, praying he was not
at lunch. Tambo answered.

'This is Harpur.'

There was not much hesitation: 'Colin. Yes. Colin, I'm
terribly sorry. I would have liked to talk at the funeral, but
not on, was it? And what was I supposed to say? Are you
going to listen to my grief?'

Harpur thought he heard the phone picked up downstairs
and then that special, extra silence given by a hand over
the mouthpiece.

'We've got a man working on your ground, sir. Sergeant
Jeremy Jones.'

'Erogenous? I remember him, of course. I haven't heard
about this.'

'In possible peril.'

'You want help for him?'

'I've asked for help. I need to be sure.'

'They'll look after it.'

'This is to do with Careen Street.'

Again there was not much hesitation, though slightly more. 'She told you about that?'

'Of course. From the first.'

'Sometimes I don't think I really knew her.'

'He's at Piccadilly Circus station. Was. You ought to go. Personally.'

'Well, I know that.'

'And tooled up. This is some moustached dark boy, a possible friend of yours. He was on the train.'

'No, no friend, Colin, believe me.'

'Not to Erogenous, anyway. But you recognize the description? Can you draw a weapon – think of a reason?'

'Always Erogenous overdid.'

When Harpur went back downstairs the girls were knocking a meal together and Scott, seated beneath the urn which Harpur recently bought, had the prayer book open on his lap. '*With my body I thee worship*,' he called out to Hazel and Jill in the kitchen. 'That's lovely, Mr Harpur – the way marriage turns people into gods and goddesses, fit for adoration.'

'It has some big powers,' Harpur replied.

Chapter 39

When they reached the theatre for *Endgame* Tambo had wanted to change the seats. This was before they had sat down in their booked places, so it could not be that he had seen anyone close. He said he preferred the circle to the stalls. So, why reserve stalls in the first place? The house was full, anyway, and no switch possible. She had suspected for a second that he would say they must abandon *Endgame* then: the same sort of blank urgency as he had shown at the Impressionists. But, in fact, he shrugged and smiled and led the way to the stalls, as if suggesting the change had been a whim only, not important. She had the idea he feared doing the predictable, and booked seats might make him predictable, though who could know about them she did not understand. Was it much more than a twitch in him? The conflict between the poised, London, hard-bark exterior and his inner jumpiness was also difficult to understand. Megan wondered whether she contributed to that jumpiness, even caused it, by giving him no settled programme for the future: just trip nine next, trip ten, and on to trip twenty, thirty, fifty? Was she fair to Tambo? Might the stress get too much one day and make him look elsewhere? She must face up, and before very long. She hardly knew how to cope with him in this state. Colin had his big worries, but she had never seen anything comparable in him.

Tambo's anxieties even reduced her pleasure in *Endgame*, usually a favourite play of hers. Tonight, it seemed to her wilfully bleak and negative: the cruel absurdity of people in dustbins, the bare set, the poverty-stricken language. To her surprise, she found herself craving costume, colour, escape. God, was that what she was, or had become – an escapist? At the flat, Tambo's unease persisted. The sex was ferocious and prolonged: like a farewell, she thought, his hands on her like someone clutching at a lifebelt.

'What's the matter?' she said.

'Perhaps we'll go back to the hotel.'

'Lovely.'

'Say some time in the New Year.'

'As soon as you like.'

'I still don't want to give offence – seem ungrateful.'

'Who'd know? The owner would think you had no more use for the flat. Love affairs come and go, Tambo. He, she, is not going to discover you've moved to somewhere else.'

'No, probably not.'

'Surely not. They've got tabs on you?'

He laughed. 'Of course not.'

'If they've got tabs on you they've got tabs on me. I don't fancy that.'

'No question of it. I just want to wind down the arrangement slowly, not seem to chuck it over.'

'We could even go to your place.'

'Oh, you wouldn't like that.'

'Well, I might. Perhaps it would be nice to see you in an ordinary, day-in day-out spot.' She still did not really think so, but this seemed a decent, constructive thing to say now, and not escapist at all. It might feel to Tambo like a move towards domesticity and permanence. Perhaps it was.

Chapter 40

Lamb said: 'Anyone missing, Col?'

It was one of those questions where you could feel a built-in answer. 'Who?' Harpur replied.

'What I'm asking. Anyone of yours missing in London?'

They were at what they called Three Rendezvous, a Home Guard blockhouse on the foreshore, with a fine view of mud flats, mixed debris, black and ginger seaweed, wrecks, beige hillocks of effluent frisky in the wind. On his way into work, Harpur had noticed Jack Lamb's Lancia Dedra sticking close behind. When Lamb saw Harpur watching him in the mirror he had raised three fingers, and Harpur turned off to here.

They stood on the sea side of the blockhouse now, cars parked well apart from each other some way off. Lamb gazed out, grey eyes trans-Continental, as if once more searching for a worthwhile, world-scourge enemy. They went inside the blockhouse only if the weather turned grim. For one thing, layered odours of decades could turn the stomach. For another, at almost all their meeting places they had to guard against being seen as a couple and arrested: the blockhouse would not rate as 'in private' if they were mistaken for consenting adults. Lamb had on a trenchcoat, brown trilby and brown ankle boots today and carried a thin walking stick. He might have been an eternally stuck captain wanting to look a briga-dier and only missing it by hitting it too right, like Robert de Niro as a boxer.

'I refused you that Careen Street address, for your safety, Col. But you found it. Clever lad, and typical. And such a risk.'

'Careen Street?' Harpur replied.

'How did you get it?' He put a mittened hand on Harpur's shoulder. 'But forgive me. Generally only you would ask such a gross question. Then you put someone to look at it? Who's missing, Col?'

Harpur felt himself begin to shake and moved away from Lamb's hand, before Jack detected it. 'What's happened?'

Lamb said: 'Obviously, I had people looking at it, too – my own interests, apart from yours. Uncontinuous, but as thorough as they can make it. I'm not a police force, just a private individual with a few London friends to work off-and-on for me, though talented. To be specific, I had one man and a kid of nineteen doing this job, looking at 26A. They were taking it turn and turn about, and, Col, I'd like you to keep that in mind, because it explains why—' His voice went bleaker: 'It explains why no rescue thing could be made. We're talking about Geraint, the London kid of nineteen, who happened to be on duty when it all happened. He can't take on three, and possibly more.'

'What three, Jack?' Jesus.

'This is a nexus address, I'd say, this 26A. We agree on that? Colin, my lad sees your lad spotted by other people at Careen Street and tracked to Piccadilly station.'

'Oh?'

'Your lad phones. One call. Phones *you*? He leaves the phone, and then an incident, obscured by crowds. Your lad is at the centre of it, very much so, hemmed in by three of them. But he's still walking afterwards. He's between two and one behind, but not being carried or even supported, that's my information. No obvious damage. My God, this is midday, a thronged station – Christmas shoppers, winos and what all. They stroll out, perhaps something unmistakable pressed against him, up past the Regent Palace to Brewer Street then into Great Pultney where there's a blue Carlton waiting. Geraint's on foot behind. The Carlton leaves up Brewer Street, your boy and the rest aboard, your boy invisible through the rear side window, but in there, shrouded again by the escorts. Yes, shrouded. The car's gone by the time Geraint who could be of Welsh stock finds a cab. There's a number, but it might be stolen, of course. Oh, of course stolen, for that kind of full-exposure job. So, which of your people, Col?' Now, it was hardly a question at all. He sounded hoarse still and was suddenly close to shouting and close to weeping. Turning for a second he pushed his vast, middle-ageing, agonized features near Harpur's but did not lower his voice: 'Early forties. Navy raincoat, pricey black shoes, navy trousers, probably a suit, good mop of dark hair, show-nothing face. This is Erogenous, for Christ's sake? You sent Erogenous alone up there, you obsessed, cruel bastard. He's gifted, yes – but on territory he doesn't know, except from the ABC?'

Harpur quelled the trembling. 'He knows the Regent Palace. He went unasked this time. I didn't send him.'

'This time? How went? How did he get the address? You sweat for vengeance for a wife you were at least two-timing, maybe more, and who was two-timing you. Why the urgency, Col?'

'Marriage.'

'Well, Erogenous wasn't married to her.'

'Where is he, Jack?'

Lamb resumed his sea watch and spoke now into the mainly brown vista. 'Sorry for the harsh words. It's guilt. Col, do you understand, I feel responsible for all this?'

'Don't.'

'I let you hear the fucking tape—'

'Yes, fucking tape.'

'How could I do it?'

'I forced you, Jack.'

'I don't get forced, and certainly not by Colin Harpur. I know all your ploys. A few climax whoops knock the reason out of you? All right, that's forgivable. You act mad. But then you make others act mad. Known as leadership, I suppose.'

'I'll have the registration, Jack. Run-downs of the three who took him? The Carlton driver?'

'Of course.' Lamb handed him a typed sheet. Glancing at it, Harpur saw in the second description the dark moustache, right age. Lamb said: 'Only two or three times I bumped into Erogenous. Grand lad. Everything I heard of him was good.

168

He thought the world of you, Col, even pre-Link Street. Then we hand him to the wild things.'

'Stuff the self-pity. Erogenous always did what he wanted.'

They began walking to the cars. 'My boy abandons the cab and goes back towards the station. It's sealed off and heavy with police, including Tambo, wearing civvies and keeping to the margin, recognized by Geraint. The cavalry was quick, but still ten minutes or more too late. You made the call? At least that's something. Col, you can ask the Met for unidentified bodies his age group and so on? Of course, they might freight Erogenous elsewhere.'

Harpur said: 'This lad of yours, he's nineteen, but he sounds informed, if he knows Tambo.'

'Of course he's informed, or would I use him? You're asking, does he recognize any of those three or the driver? Can we get a possible location for Erogenous that way?'

'That's it, Jack. Can we? And in time.'

'They'll want to talk to Erogenous, won't they? Get the story? Really talk to him.'

'Yes, they will.'

'That could – he might hold out.'

'Yes. He will.'

'For a while. Geraint didn't know any of them. But we're asking around, naturally. Really working at it.' They were at a spot where they would separate and go to their cars. Lamb said: 'Col, this is delicate again.'

'Go ahead.'

'We have, of course, the connection between Tambo and the flat.'

'Of course.'

'And these people are connected with the flat. Tambo would probably know some of them, even all.'

'It's possible.'

'Couldn't he be the way to find Erogenous? In time.'

'He could be.'

Lamb groaned. 'But he can't admit he knows any of them, because he shouldn't, and if he acts he's lifting the lid on a dirty life? His?'

'This is possible, Jack.'

'Christ, he's going to sit on something like that? He knows what happened? You'd called him? Why he was there?'

'He knows *something* has happened.'

'He's not in touch with you?'

'He was my wife's lover, Jack. Perhaps she was due to go to him permanently. We don't fraternize. I'd be keen to hear from you. Anything at all you get. Tell me, Jack. And no unaccompanied London trips.'

'Helen's been gassing to you?'

'Talk to me if you hear something.' Harpur resumed his journey to work.

Mid-morning, Iles and Garland came into his room and sat down. He was looking at the updated countrywide male corpse list, concentrating on London. No Erogenous. It was early yet. The computer said the Carlton had been stolen in Surrey a fortnight before.

Iles must have a Christmas function today and looked a picture in the blue uniform. 'I've had to move delicately on the frozen fish, Colin,' he said. 'Some hick cop like me or Francis start asking Lower Bond Street grocers who buys their stuff and one of them might ring the Yard to check authority. Tambo would hear. I keep in mind he's tied to all this somehow – somehow meaning on the take. I'd rather he didn't know where we're operating.'

In that clipped, off-hand way he had when triumphal, Garland said, 'What we discovered rather roundabout from the shop is that a dark-haired, dark-moustached lad, twenty-fiveish, sometimes in a fur-collared dark astrakhan or mohair overcoat, would come in regularly and buy half a dozen or a dozen of these meals.'

'Paying cash,' Harpur replied.

'Paying cash,' Garland said.

'Francis has done a passable job on this, without, as far as we know, starting any bells. Tranquillize his dick for say thirty-six hours and he will give gifted moments to detective arts. You'll get the resemblance to our train friend, Col?' Iles said.

'Where does it take us?' Harpur replied.

'We could wait for him to come back to the shop. I'd suppose stocking some town flat, *pied-à-terre*, in the vicinity,' Iles said. 'That's a lot of front doors. He might lead us.' He smiled nicely at Harpur. 'My feeling is, you have this address already, you see, Col. I'm wasting my time?'

Garland said: 'Then we ask, why was Megan carrying the damn stuff home with her.'

'Yes,' Harpur replied.

'Jesus, I've told you that,' Iles answered. 'Tambo thinks best not snub the heavy benefactor.'

'He was always a diplomat,' Harpur said.

'Women went for that,' Iles stated. 'But I don't have to tell you, Col.'

'I say again, too simple, sir,' Garland replied. He was in a suit today, perhaps to seem right in Lower Bond Street. The crew-cut did not chime too well, but Francis had the cheek to win most people, at least short-term. Like Iles, he did not look police: both had a mildness and delicacy to their features that Harpur envied, because with these came the ability to lull and lead people on before clobbering them. With his face and build, Harpur had to go at things more head-on early. Subtlety he lusted for.

'Yes, OK, Francis, sod off,' Iles remarked. 'Knock down my reading but supply none.' Harpur was still behind his desk with the deads list folded over. Iles smiled at him again, now a collegiate, genial, wholly trustworthy smile, so Harpur prepared for a full shit blitz. 'Yes, Col, as I see it, I'm sitting here, proud of my sad fragments of progress, and Garland's, and, of course, all the time we know we're seven leagues behind you and no special boots to catch up. We thrill over convenience halibut and you're almost ready to nail the whole bloody lot of them, including Tambo. And then Erogenous missing. I have Jane Something, his lady, on this morning, worried and wanting a trace. What's this about, Col? What are you two at?'

'Erogenous?' Harpur replied.

Rage ravaged Iles's gentle features for a second. 'Oh, save it,' he grunted. 'He's offering special services for a promotion boost? I hear they're giving it to him, anyway. One put in a word for him one's self. He kicks over, yes, but I've come to think we'll only win that way. So, sure, Inspector Erogenous Jones. But where is he?'

Harpur said: 'He does drop out of sight now and then, if

he's into something good. I've got him on the warehouse robberies.'

Iles stood. 'Bollocks. Stewed bollocks, Harpur. Col, have you thought I'll be going back now to dear Roger and Coral to give them pressure about this moustache and fur collar they happened never to see on the train? If I find they talked to you privately and you've kept it all on deposit, you're finished, you crass, dissembling jerk, aren't you? How could even you survive that, Harpur? Don't think Daddy Lane could save you, even at his most priestly and soulful. Consider: you have two daughters to support, who will need quality wedding receptions with tolerable wines and vol-aux-vents out of your pocket. You should have given that some responsible thought, shouldn't you? Hazel would marry that Scott eventually? Coral I really feel like working on, searching for yield.'

'Sir, I heard you've already accomplished wonders with Mrs Grant, and Scott will be at your place for Christmas after all,' Harpur replied. 'Hazel's so delighted.'

'Ah. Delighted. Honestly? Good. What I mean, Scott's a nice kid, but doesn't she find him a bit of a—?'

'Kid?' Harpur replied. 'She's a kid herself, sir.'

'Not disablingly so. Scott's mother? She turns out to be a very receptive lady,' Iles said. 'Ready to come much more than half-way to meet one as long as one shows respect for her dignity, fashion sense and mind and that, and doesn't just start slam-bang, straight in. Yes, indeed, Sarah and I are so looking forward to a lovely, warm Christmas gathering, everyone happy and mindful of what this supreme occasion is about. That's the crucial thing. Then the sheer good fellowship, the happy sense of belonging. Francis, do you want to attend, with companion, of course, as long as she-he washes under the arms? You're still hetero? I pry only so we can alternate gender placings at the table, on which Sarah's fussy. I would have asked earlier but had to mull over at length whether I really wanted a thin-lipped arrogant prat like you present on such a goodly occasion. But, obviously, Harpur will be there, so why not another who's had my wife? Christmas is hardly a time for mean spirits, surely.'

'Thanks so much, sir,' Garland replied. 'It's very kind, but I always go to my mother's.'

'How sweet,' Iles said. 'I've heard of people like that. Family bonds. Careful with your dear little teeth if she puts coins in the pudding.'

Chapter 41

Returning on the last train after Trip Eight, the *Endgame* outing, Megan had had the absurd feeling that she would like to discuss Tambo's behaviour with Colin. The habits of marriage were hard to drop: you chewed over your big problems with the spouse, and Tambo was suddenly a big problem. But, obviously, not one she would be asking Colin about: *Col, lover boy seems to be getting ragged around the edges. What should I do? Leave you and take permanent comfort to him? He's short of moral ballast, poor dear.*

She longed to discuss Tambo's frightening symptoms with an expert: that is, with another cop, and especially a long-time grey-area cop like her husband. She would list to him the business over the theatre seats tonight, and the seeming turmoil about the Careen Street place, and the crisis at the Impressionist exhibition last time. *What does it add up to, Col?* She had her own idea of what it added up to, but she was only a police wife, not a full licentiate of this shady guild of craftsmen.

The point was that, even if she put all this to Colin, and even though it concerned someone he might want to injure, the chances were that he would listen to her, silently, instantly formulating his exact interpretation, and reply that he really did not know what to make of it all, and would need harder information before reaching even a tentative opinion. He would talk such elevated, moot-point crap when determined to hand her off. And on any dubious police practice, he was determined to hand her off.

My own reading, for what it's worth, Col, is that he has involved himself in a dirty partnership with big, dirty people

*for gain and possibly wants to get out of it now, but can't.
Only big people could provide that flat. It might also be that
he does not want yours truly seen with him regularly because
this could put me at hazard, if things get really bitter. That
kind of gallant impulse in a grubby context would, I believe,
be natural to Tambo.*

This might be blunt enough to draw Colin finally into some
sort of committed response, such as 'Really?' or even 'Policing
is a tricky game.' He would be hearing none of it, though.
Impossible.

When the train pulled in and she had walked to her car, she
found herself feeling glad to be home – safer, cleaner, back
from the land of the hellishly stressed. She despised this
reaction. It was bourgeois, provincial, meagre-minded, all
tendencies she was brought up to be sniffy about and *was*
sniffy about, she hoped. What had happened to the demands
for freedom, fun, expansiveness? She was bolting back grate-
fully to the family fortress in the sticks, cowed, gutless, rather
ordinary. Of course, she would go up again, and soon: the
Christmas shopping pretext. Tonight, though, she had felt she'd
had enough of London for a while.

Chapter 42

'So are you Welsh, Geraint?' Harpur asked.

'How's that?'

'Geraint – it's some fine Welsh knight or prince in history, yes?'

'A road in Bromley, Kent. My father painted a house there.'

'What you get for asking background, Col,' Lamb said. 'We'll go in, Geraint. You stay with the car and ready to hot tail.'

'You? I found this fucking place, you know. Didn't I go back to Careen Street for you, Jack, spot the moustache man again, and this time stick with him, not lose the sod at Piccadilly Circus? Then I trace him here. Subsequently, you get duly notified and can bring your Harpur friend.'

'Brilliant. But the driving's as important as any of it, and maybe more,' Lamb replied.

'Yes, more,' Harpur said. 'Plus sentry.'

'So, if there's trouble?' Geraint replied.

'I'd say if there's trouble quit. Vamoose. Leave us to it. But I know you won't,' Lamb said.

'No, the bugger won't,' Dale said.

'Or just dial 999 and say an incident,' Harpur told him.

'Talk to police?' Geraint snarled.

'No name,' Lamb said. 'Anyway, what do you think *he* is?'

'You get trouble, perhaps I'll come in,' Geraint replied.

'Yes, perhaps you will,' Dale said.

'Well, with some subtlety,' Lamb said.

'What's that mean?' Geraint asked.

'Someone up a ladder spots a street name for his baby boy must obviously think a lot of him,' Harpur replied. 'Jack has to take care of you, Geraint, on your dad's behalf.'

'Exactly,' Lamb said. 'Oh, move all the time with your back to a wall and don't neon yourself against windows. The usual. Trap shut and quiet breathing. That stuff about the inside of a strange house the most dangerous place on earth.'

Geraint leaned across from behind the wheel and stuck his big, bony face close to Lamb's, the kind of approach Jack sometimes used himself: 'Jesus, don't I know subtlety? Subtlety's my soul. What else brings us here, for fuck's sake? How do I pick up this moustache on another Careen Street visit, follow him home to his Southall place, get an ID, then tail him here to Peckham unseen?'

'You sure unseen?' Harpur asked. 'Yes, that's subtle. As bright as anything Erogenous himself could do.'

'I haven't seen no brightness in that one,' Geraint said. 'Cornered at Piccadilly, that's all. Think he's alive in here?'

'I'd say three to one,' Dale replied. 'Against. In view of what we know now of the moustache – Mr Clive Thomas Brince, as gorgeous Geraint discovers from the Southall neighbours – and who he works for.'

'Christ, no,' Harpur yelled. 'Better than that. Much. Better than evens. This is London, not Detroit. Who kills police here?'

'Worked up? So, he's a friend, not just another copper?' Geraint replied.

'Both,' Harpur said. 'It's not impossible.'

'You people look after each other,' Geraint replied. 'There's a word for it.'

'Some of us do, up to a point,' Harpur said.

'And you owe?'

'Absolutely.'

'Canteen culture,' Lamb said. 'All games have that.'

'You've got fire power?' Geraint asked.

'I couldn't draw police armament, for God's sake,' Harpur said.

'It's private?' Geraint said. 'Why we're in my car?'

'It's private.'

'Get a private piece then.'

'I'm a temporary immigrant on Metropolitan Police ground,

Geraint. I can't risk shooting. It would be held against eternally, and I'd never make HM Inspectorate. You can square a lot of grievances in that job.'

'But moustache, and so on?' Geraint asked. 'Weapons?'

'They might have something.'

'Shit. We're supposed to be sweet and subtle instead? They could have us marked already, four ugly buggers waiting in a car, which could be why no lights in there. And two ugly buggers watching before that.'

'Speak for your bloody self,' Dale said. 'I've had girls imploring me, and not rubbish.'

'What about you, Jack, Dale? You equipped?'

'How would I carry working with police?' Dale chuckled. 'The sods do you for possession when you only fired to save them.'

'Right,' Lamb said.

'I've got finger irons and a little metal cosh my mother made me,' Harpur said.

'So are you serious about bringing this what's-his-name out?' Geraint asked.

'Erogenous. Very,' Harpur said. 'Christmas wouldn't be Christmas without.'

The old orange-brown Princess was spacious. Geraint stretched, straightening his stork legs under the fascia and reaching up behind him to touch the grimy, off-grey ceiling above Harpur, in the back with Dale and Geraint's groceries. There was a rich smell of petrol and Christmas sprouts. Geraint had big, knobbly, unsubtle hands which he held on the ceiling for a while splayed. Hands like that could have been useful for a Welsh knight fighting boars with a lance. But the hands and Geraint overall reminded Harpur more of a gawky, suffering character called Smike, illustrated in one of the three or four books at home when he was a kid. The book did a lot on cruelty to children and Harpur wondered if his parents kept it available so he could see things might be much worse, and would be if he did not watch it. Yawning, Geraint said to Harpur: 'Look, Jack pays me and Dale. You pay Jack?'

'There's what's called a mutual understanding,' Lamb replied.

'This is an understanding from way, way back, Geraint,' Harpur said.

'I see what Jack does for you,' Geraint said, flapping a bumpy wrist towards the house they somehow had to get into soon. 'What do you do for him?'

'Yes, an understanding from way, way back, Smike – I mean, Geraint,' Harpur replied. 'You carry something?'

'Smike? Who's Smike? Finger whistle if you're up against,' Geraint replied. 'Or if I see someone come in I'll follow.'

'Is this always OK for starting?' Lamb said.

'I had the battery on feed overnight twice,' Geraint replied.

'It sounded bonny,' Harpur said.

'Like we agreed, we'll disperse, Geraint,' Lamb said. 'Mr Harpur and Dale come back with Erogenous to the car. I walk and look for a cab. It mucks up tracing.'

'Five-figure reward, maybe, for saving a cop?' Geraint replied. 'Even an out-of-town cop. I could trade up the car a year or two.'

'Right into the 1980s, you mean?' Dale said.

'No reward. I told you it's private,' Harpur replied.

'They'd write off one of their own boys?'

The three of them left the car. It was a street of big, four-storeyed Victorian houses, all flatted and a hearty ethnic mix. Probably this had been a fine road once, full of management and the higher teachers. Geraint said he tailed Clive Thomas Brince, the moustache, from Southall to the basement of 13, a property with the name Palmerston on a coloured glass panel over the front door. Harpur wouldn't have minded one of his gunboats. The basement was not lit, and Geraint and Dale reported there had been no movement in or near it since Brince left this morning. Or no movement they had seen. It was Christmas Eve.

They had walked a couple of steps when Geraint tapped the driver's window and rolled it down as Harpur turned back. 'Anyway, we're saving nobody. At the Circus he looked like an all-times victim,' Geraint said. 'I'll up it to five to one he's not alive. Twenties? Jack to hold the money.'

'Piss off, Geraint,' Harpur replied, but he called Lamb and handed him the twenty, then waited to see Geraint give him a hundred. Geraint pulled the money in a loose sheaf of tens from the breast pocket of his big-shoulder, green-grey suit that could hide anything, except Geraint's obvious quality.

There were eight steps to the basement. Harpur and Dale went down, while Jack looked for a back entrance. The steps were surprisingly spruce, no street debris and a couple of potted ferns set at alternate ends of each. The area around the front door was similarly clean and tidy with more evergreen horticulture in pots, and Harpur began to wonder whether Geraint and Dale had it right. The place was beginning to feel like someone's nicely cared for, rather characterful home, even a woman's. It was just after 4.30 p.m., completely dark, but still no lights came on in the basement. 'How are you with locks?' Harpur asked.

Dale shook his head and let a small jemmy slip into his hand from where it had nestled up his sleeve. 'Doubles as weapon and key,' he said. Dale would be on his way to forty, almost middle-class accent, dark hair greying, cheery, inquisitive face, heavy spectacles, ragged teeth, a shapeless old tweed overcoat with good, big square pockets for job aids. To Harpur he looked like one of the long-term unemployed and loving it, but Harpur knew that in quick character assessments he often leaned towards the fascist. Dale shoved the metal tongue behind the Yale and levered feelingly. He might not offer any magic touch but he knew how to take a bit of care. Harpur brought the pencil flashlight from his pocket ready and touched the shaft of his savage revered baby cosh, just checking. It seemed wrong to be fondling such a cruel instrument in this dinky urban arbour and you could say the same about ripping the woodwork to pieces. He had the knuckle-duster on his flashlight hand.

Dale pushed the door back gently with the end of the jemmy, then kept it ready in his right. They stood quietly for a few moments, listening and trying to shut out traffic noise and resident noise from the upper storeys: voices, some music, a baby, kitchen sounds. Illicit entry to property almost always thrilled Harpur, brought him the kind of deep gladness some derived from church music or Masonry or the birth of a child. You were sliding into people's privacies, deducing their souls from possessions, décor, papers, and this was often so much more spot-on than what they told you, and often so much more spot-on than what they genuinely believed about themselves, the dim sods. Intrusion in a good cause he considered as just like psychiatry. The doctor looked at and behind the furniture of a mind, Harpur looked at and behind the furniture. This evening, though, he did not feel the usual delight. He disliked company. These inner areas talked to him best when he went solitary: like a preference for private, not public, prayer. Plus, he was in terror of what he would discover here, meaning not opposition but Erogenous dumped and dead. Psychiatrists had it easy and were never forced to face that sort of agony and that sort of guilt. He might need one if things here turned out bad.

They went inside, Harpur leading, and waited again, still in the dark. Geraint was right, and that aged vehicle and its contents must be noticeable. Dale had been reasonably delicate with the door, but the noise would have carried, even above all the neighbour din. People could be waiting. All the same, what Harpur wanted to do now, straight off to ease his worries, was call, bellow, Erogenous's name – his real name, in those strained, formal circumstances, Jeremy Stanislaus Jones. It would have been as mad as switching on the flashlight. If Erogenous were here and alone and capable of it he would call, bellow himself, knowing a break-in must mean help. But the call did not come. Perhaps occasionally Harpur heard a strange insistent grunting, though that could be coming from anywhere – humping in another flat, or the plumbing.

A small, square hall. There was a pleasant, lively smell, which comforted Harpur, and he could make out more potted plants against a wall, some in good flower. A couple of doors would lead into the rest of the flat, both shut. Harpur decided it could not matter much which they tried and he was moving forward slowly to the one on his left when he thought he caught a light sound on the basement steps behind him. Dale had heard it, too, and turned fast, the jemmy up. He seemed a capable lad on basics.

Geraint appeared in the doorway, holding what looked to Harpur like a P225 eight-round SIG-Sauers pistol, a handsome job, even backed by that hand, but Christ. 'Someone moving at the back,' Geraint said at more or less full voice.

Dale got a free palm across Geraint's mouth and kept it there. Harpur put his lips to Geraint's outsize ear and whispered: 'It's Jack at the back. We told you we were doing that. Someone big?'

Dale removed his hand slowly from Geraint's mouth and let it fall to the gun wrist instead, pushing the weapon down so the P225 was pointing at the ground, not at Harpur. 'Could be big,' Geraint replied, whispering now.

'Yes, it's Jack,' Harpur replied.

'Well, I'm here, anyway,' Geraint said.

'We've got no watch on the street,' Harpur replied.

'It's quiet. Nobody's going to pinch the Princess.'

'Get back up there, Geraint,' Dale said.

'You look like a couple of learners,' Geraint replied. 'Iron bar and finger fittings. Hanging about.' He was talking almost at normal again.

Dale took Geraint by the arm and tried to turn him towards the steps. Geraint pulled away. He did not raise the gun but Harpur had an idea he thought about it. Dale must also have had the idea because he tried no more persuasion. Geraint went forward, stood against the wall out of the line of fire from inside and suddenly banged open one of the doors. It could have been done slightly better, but not much, and only by Robert Stack. Possibly, Geraint was less than a total arsehole and, as he said, had found this place and put a name to Mr Moustache via the Southall neighbours – more than Harpur had managed, or Iles, at least as far as was known. Harpur could just about see Geraint raise the gun, take a two-hand grip and go fast into the room beyond, half crouched, the P225 out in front. It was a copybook urban warfare move, as seen on TV. Harpur went in smartly behind him, ready to knock Geraint sideways and unconscious with the hand irons if he seemed like firing, because in the dark he would probably fire at anything that moved, including Erogenous, and not just to make his bet safe. If it had been light he would probably fire at anything that moved, too.

It appeared to be a curtained sitting-room and now Harpur

did risk the flashlight, moving its thin beam slowly around. He was conscious of Geraint following it with the pistol. The room looked serene, chintzy, lived-in but lived in decorously, the kind of room his mother would have liked but never had. He saw a three-piece moquette suite, a mock-coal electric fire, a thirties or forties bureau and some blue sea, blue sky, China-clipper type prints in big gold frames on the walls. Harpur yearned to get at the bureau, but this was not why they had come. He delighted in desks and the prospect of life policies and shopping lists and cheque stubs and supposed secret drawers. There was a half-open door at the far end, and when Harpur risked the beam on that he saw a stove and dresser full of crockery.

He never expected joy in kitchens and, turning, went back into the hall and opened the other door there, pretty much as Geraint had done, but without gun-play. He kept the flashlight on, though, and almost immediately saw Erogenous. His first thought was, the loon with the SIG-Sauer, and he shouted, really shouted and to hell with secrecy: 'He's here and you're a fucking century down, Smike.'

'What's this bloody Smike?' Geraint said.

'Geraint,' Harpur replied.

'So what's this bloody Smike?'

'Mike,' Harpur said. 'You remind me of a stupendously talented kid called Mike.'

'It sounded like Smike.'

'What the hell would Smike be?' Harpur asked. 'This is Inspector Jones, Geraint, Dale.'

It was a bedroom, in the same style as the living-room, with a couple of unmade single beds. That untidiness shocked Harpur after what they had grown used to. Heavy blue curtains were drawn. On the far side of the room, a charming piece of floral Wilton carpet had been rolled back exposing a heavy safe let into the floor, where a square section of the board had been removed. The wood square stood against the wardrobe. The safe had a thick metal handle, to make it easy to pull open when bending over. The safe seemed to be locked. Erogenous, naked, was manacled to the handle with two sets of padlocked chains, right wrist to right ankle, left wrist to left ankle. He was lying on his side facing the door, perhaps had turned that way on hearing the noise. His mouth was taped, which would account for the grunting. He had scars more or less all over, and Harpur could not be sure in this light whether they were bruises or burns. No: he could not be sure which were bruises and which were burns. Geraint switched the lights on. 'Jesus', he said. 'I'm glad to lose.'

Harpur went forward and eased the tape off. 'Did you say Inspector?' Erogenous asked.

'Of course.'

'I gave them your name, Colin,' he said. 'But not till the second day, and not till late. And address. And the kids' names.'

'Of course you did. I'd have given them yours, or anyone else's.'

'They think we're into exposing some business partnership involving—'

'We are. But I've got some helpers with me, Erogenous,' Harpur replied.

'Right. They'll come back. Give me a piss and so on, feed and water me, work on me. Your kids etcetera going to be all right?'

'I might give Iles a ring. There's no need for secrecy now.'

'But you like secrecy,' Erogenous replied. 'You want to keep wife stuff close, don't you?'

'Yes.'

'And you sure you want Iles near your kids, the older one? Well, at least the older one.'

'It's a point,' Harpur replied. 'I'll call Francis. Will you have a look at the rest of the place, Geraint? Don't kill Jack, coming in from the rear, you might damage the bet stake.'

'You look, Dale,' Geraint said. He handed him the pistol, and Dale took it and put the jemmy into one of his big pockets. Geraint said: 'I'd better do the locks, unless you can, Harpur?'

'No.'

'No. Not so smartarse now.' Geraint folded the skinny, awkward body down alongside Erogenous and gazed at the locks for a while. They were strong and sophisticated-looking items. After a while, Geraint produced from his jacket pocket a folding plastic wallet which held about thirty three-inch

184

pieces of metal under short elastic straps, like a set of make-up aids for someone with a hefty range of faults to work on. The pieces of metal had key ends but no handles. Perhaps he could argue they were not keys if he was patrol stopped and done for kitted for burglary. Perhaps. Geraint removed all thirty from their places and swiftly laid them out in an immaculate line on the boards, a two-inch space between each. He took Harpur's flashlight, then crouched lower so he could point its beam at the keyhole of the lock on Erogenous's left wrist and ankle, and stared into it with one eye from half an inch away, like a doctor doing tonsils, an ugly doctor, but then most were. He stayed in that position, not moving for about thirty seconds, then reached out with his huge, lumpy hand and felt systematically along the bits of metal, starting at number one and going right through, never disturbing their positions, never looking at them. He gave each a swift but thorough charting with his finger tips. Occasionally he paused and went back over a piece. When he had reached the end, he returned his hand to one of the pieces he had fiddled with most. One eye still closed, the other squinting at the lock's innards, he now played his fingers over the key end of this piece and the two after it. From the third of them he went back to the first of this trio and did the drill on each again. Finally, he chose the third and sat up straight with it between his fingers. For the first time he glanced at the piece he had picked. He fitted it in the lock which opened immediately. Erogenous whooped and rubbed Geraint's hair in congratulation. 'You've missed your vocation, kid. You should have been a robber,' he said.

Geraint said: 'That right?' Now he did a similar close up of the second lock.

'Not the same?' Harpur asked.

'How stupid can you get, Chief Superintendent?' Geraint replied. 'What's the point of securing something twice if there's a single way of undoing it?'

He went through the same rigmarole, but this time on his first try picked the wrong key. The right one turned out to be second on his shortlist. 'My fingers are coarsening with age,' Geraint said.

Dale had returned. 'Wanking,' he said. 'Here's Jack and a

guest.' When Harpur looked he saw Dale had the pistol jammed against Tambo, who was in a yellow duffle coat and black bobble hat, and wore heavy walking boots.

'That's the lad I saw lurking at the back,' Geraint said. 'I know him, obviously.'

'So now let's see you open the safe, wonder-kid,' Dale replied. 'He does his brain surgery act on a couple of job-lot padlocks, but how about a decent challenge? We might find a bonus.'

'Where are your clothes, Erog?' Harpur asked. 'It's cold.'

'Well, yes,' Erogenous said. 'I don't know. They went through them.'

'Have a look in the wardrobe, Dale,' Harpur said.

'What about him?' He prodded Tambo with the gun.

'He's all right,' Harpur replied.

'More police?'

'A colleague, yes,' Harpur said.

'Another friend?' Geraint asked.

'A colleague,' Harpur said.

'You hate him for something?' Geraint asked.

'A colleague,' Harpur said.

'What, fucking your wife or something? Bowled you for a duck in the inter-Force tourney?' Geraint replied.

'In an important job up here,' Harpur said.

'You don't say. How come we didn't know about him showing here?' Geraint replied. He was on the floor again, this time listening to the tumblers while he talked, and playing with the safe's combination mechanism.

'We've approached this thing from different directions, that's all,' Harpur said.

'Yes,' Tambo replied.

'Which thing is that?' Geraint asked. 'Your wife? She liked it from different directions?'

Tambo looked pretty bad, Harpur thought, the good features still good, obviously – good enough for him to be Tamburlaine again if called – but his chin and mouth slack. He had had some foul pressure, and maybe some frights.

'I hoped Erogenous might be here,' Tambo said.

'You had this address?' Geraint asked. 'You're smarter than Harpur.'

'Some think so,' Harpur said.

'It's not so hard to be that,' Geraint replied. 'He wouldn't balls up my name and call me something from *Nick Nickleby.*'

'I was scared for Erogenous,' Tambo replied.

'So, you know the people who were holding him?' Geraint asked from the floor. 'What they could do to him? How did you know that? You're confeds with them? Got the address that way?'

Dale came back from the wardrobe with what looked like a sable fur coat, full length. 'This is all,' he said. 'She's scared to wear it, whoever she is, because of the animal lobby.' Erogenous put the coat on and held it around him, savouring the warmth, but wincing also, as the material sat on his wounds. It came to just above his ankles.

'I've got wellingtons in the car boot, so you'll be fine,' Geraint said. He pulled open the safe. It was empty.

'Can I talk to you alone for a minute, Colin?' Tambo said.

'We need to get out of here quite fast,' Harpur replied.

'This is business, is it?' Geraint asked. 'The underside. Why not? We'll get Erogenous to the car. I'll give you three minutes.'

'I'll go, too,' Lamb said, 'as agreed.'

'But pay him his winnings,' Geraint replied.

'What was that about?' Erogenous asked.

'No, give it to Geraint, Jack,' Harpur said.

'Fuck off, Harpur,' Geraint replied. 'I don't take favours from police.' Lamb handed Harpur the £120.

When they had gone, Tambo and Harpur stood in the dark in the tidy living room. 'What will you do?' Tambo asked.

'I ought to put Iles on to Brince.'

'Not till you get back?'

'If I do, when I get back, yes. Tomorrow. A Christmas party at Iles's place. I'll probably risk it then when he might be genial – reveal what I've been holding back. It's tricky.'

'Thanks, Colin,' Tambo said. 'The delay could be useful. I came tonight looking for Erogenous, yes, but meaning to free myself, too. You understand?

'A bit.'

'To free myself if I could and—' He stopped briefly. 'This is arrogant?'

'To see to things for Megan?'

'She was still yours.'

'Somehow, I want him at Careen Street, not here.'

Again Tambo stayed quiet for a second. 'Yes, I suppose so.'

'After Christmas, I expect,' Harpur said. 'If I don't tell Iles. Anyway, what do I want Brince for? He was only on orders. I want who sent him.'

'Impossible. Please, believe that. You take what's on offer, Colin. That's policing. Brince is. I came down after her you know, that night. Drove. I was too late. Clearly.'

'I remember a car.'

'Yes, you were in the headlights, holding her. I decided then I shouldn't interfere. Had no right. Marriage is marriage.'

'Right. Why did you follow? Did you see somebody go for the train after her? Why didn't you get the guard phoned, for God's sake? They're reachable on most trains. But you wanted no fuss.'

'It could be that. I didn't decide to come until more than an hour after the train left. Christ, a disaster. My fault. I need to put it to rights, Colin.' Harpur moved towards the door. 'What's Lamb here for, Colin?'

'Oh, he thinks he's hurt me. Wants to recompense, too.'

'Hurt you how?'

'Some business matter.'

'Is he still hanging about as well, waiting for him?'

'That wasn't the plan.'

'But is he?'

'It's possible.'

'Of course it's bloody possible,' Tambo said.

'Well, lock up when you leave, sir,' Harpur replied.

It was heartening and distinctive to be travelling in the back of a big car with someone wearing a long sable coat, even though it was Erogenous, and even though the car was this coughing heap.

Dale said: 'Go to my place. I've got some gear that will fit him. I'll take the coat, though there's no money in fur nowadays because of the lobby.'

'And quite right,' Geraint replied.

Chapter 43

Hazel said: 'I think there's someone, a man, at the bottom of the garden.'

Harpur was standing on a chair in the living-room, banging in a picture nail with the heel of one of Megan's shoes, to hang the framed print which had been in his Christmas parcel from Denise. The girls wanted it to replace the Pointer abstract, but he would not allow that, yet, and put the print alongside. He was wearing his Prince of Wales check suit, ready to go to Iles's for the party. The girls had slept late and were sitting on the floor near the french windows, opening their presents. They continued with that, but Jill said: 'I don't see anyone.'

'Among the trees and rhododendron bushes, Dad,' Hazel replied, holding a new denim jacket up by the shoulders in front of her, while still looking down the garden. 'God, it makes me think of Mummy in the car park, except it's day.' Her voice cracked for a moment. 'Deceitful trees.'

'No such species,' Jill said.

Harpur straightened the print. It said on the back, *Clown by Henry Miller, 1966* and was a dreamy-looking face with blueish nose under a three-cornered, black, tasselled hat. Harpur thought he liked it. Jill had heard of Henry Miller, apparently. Harpur was not asked who bought it for him and he had not said. 'What sort of man?'

'Only a glimpse. Dark overcoat. Dark hat. He might have seen me – pulled back among the bushes and trees.'

'Nothing about the face?' Harpur said. Was this the follow-up to what Erogenous had told Brince about him and the kids? These people worked Christmas Day? These people worked fast? Perhaps they would work any day and fast to stem a leak

190

about their juicy deal with Tambo. Did the bare fragments Harpur knew add up to a leak?

'I didn't see his face. He was turned the other way.'

'Hair?'

'I said a hat.' Hazel started to cry a little.

'Ease up, Dad,' Jill said.

'Yes, sorry,' Harpur replied. He stepped down from the chair, still holding the shoe, and stood back to admire the print. Clown had on a big collar and nice subdued green, brown and black motley. He was making a circle with the thumb and first finger of his left hand, possibly about to give himself a coke sniff before funny-walking into the ring for giggles. Jill said Miller knew Paris low-life.

'I could be wrong,' Hazel muttered.

Harpur strolled over and bent to admire the girls' presents. Nothing would do as a weapon, except possibly a pressurized hair-lacquer spray or the lumpy Walkman he had been badgered by Jill into getting her, still in red sledge and bells wrapping paper.

'Say exactly where.'

'The bushes between the eucalyptus and the beech,' Hazel replied.

'Imagination?' Jill said.

'Are you carrying anything, Dad?' Hazel asked.

'What do you mean?'

'You know – *anything*,' Hazel said.

'I'm carrying this shoe,' Harpur replied. That's what British policing was about. He straightened and with his free hand quickly unlocked the french windows. 'Move away from the glass now, OK? If anything goes a bit wrong get on the phone to Iles, and tell him to come and wear his fangs.' He walked swiftly down the garden, Megan's ochre high heel at his side. The daftness of the weapon reminded of him the night he went prowling through the house carrying Megan's parasol. She had been an armoury.

Looking terrible, even for him, Mark Lane, the Chief, appeared at the side of the beech, wearing the quite decent dark overcoat he had on in the car park the morning Megan was found, plus a navy fedora, and said in a voice full of agony and disintegration: 'I had to see you, Colin, face to face. I haven't been in touch with the ACC yet. It's not a phone matter, and I didn't want to disturb your girls, today especially.'

'Merry Christmas, sir,' Harpur replied. 'Perhaps we'll be able to go into the house in a minute, though.'

'To do with Tambo,' the Chief said. 'Appalling. Tell me, Colin, I'm wrong, alarmist, to see these things as indicative of a tumble into universal disorder, into, indeed, evil? Please.'

'Tambo, sir? What exactly?'

'A good friend at the Yard rang me personally at home, scrambled, before it's general knowledge. Perhaps he knew it was – well, in a sense sensitive, Colin. Gossip? It gets around, regrettably. So, an early warning for which we can all in a sense feel gratitude in view of its sensitivity.'

Lane would get into toils with words when things were in a sense sensitive. 'Yes, sir,' Harpur replied.

'Tambo's been found dead, at first sight, at this stage, suicide.'

Harpur felt no noticeable shock and nominal sorrow: wondered whether he might have been able to predict this end for Tambo if he had bothered to think much about him. 'You doubt suicide, sir?'

'Face-up on a bed, an issue Smith and Wesson Magnum still in his right hand, one round only fired. Bad, Colin, bad.' Lane seemed to mean bad for policemanship and the future of Mankind, and some might agree.

'This was at home, sir?'

'No, no, a luxury place in the West End belonging to some high-fly villain. Careen Street? Colin, a fruity setting.' Lane set off as if wanting to get to the house and the company of the girls, so no more of this terrible conversation would be possible. Then he came back.

'I think I've heard of it,' Harpur said.

'The flat?'

'The street, sir.'

'How would he have access to a place like that, Colin?'

'Access? Regularly?'

'They think it's bugged. There's possibly an archive on what he's been at in there previously, I fear. Tambo had the keys on him.'

'But alone at the apartment this time?'

'Apparently,' Lane said. 'It's a den heavy with champagne, convenience foods and – well, you'll forgive me, Col, but condoms. How some live. The whisper is Tambo was tangled in something foully dark, wanted to get out and couldn't. Except this sad way.'

It was a bright morning and the sun put almost a shine on Lane's standard pallor. You often had the feel when talking to him that he did not believe all you said or even much of it but longed to, out of niceness and hopes of a quiet life. There had been a time when he was a brilliant and aggressive detective on a neighbouring patch, and Harpur had worked with him occasionally then, and enjoyed it, learned from it. Strangely, the big job appeared to have softened him. His round brown eyes in his round doughy face had become what Iles termed 'fatally humane'. Now and then, Lane's brain and his good scepticism still flashed, but in crisis he seemed reluctant to use them flat out. Iles also remarked once that the Chief had caught benevolence, as many people, 'including, signally, one's self, Col', caught crabs.

Lane said dolefully: 'Someone in the apartment block heard the shot and dialled police. The flat's company owned, and the Yard traced two directors. A man called Anstical the chief? Seemingly a very big-time shady up there – import business, of banned substances, and highest class fencing and laundering. Some questions now certainly have to be asked about Tambo's connection with him. How could they have been above board, Colin? How?' It was almost a shriek, and Harpur saw Hazel, inside the house, turn and stare down towards the sound. 'Anstical has convinced them he knows nothing and is well alibied for the relevant times. They're trying to get the bug tapes out of him, but, of course, he knows what happened to Nixon – says they're only for business eavesdropping and are wiped immediately. Whatever happens, they think he's been given a fright and won't risk anything for a long while.'

Hazel and Jill were coming slowly down the garden carrying fire-irons and looking very frightened. Harpur went out from among the tall bushes. 'It's all right, kids. Only Mr Lane. He was on an early morning Yule walk and very kindly looked in to surprise us.'

'Not quite Father Christmas,' Lane said, 'but the best I can do.'

'Through our garden?' Hazel said.

'My chimney days are over,' Lane replied. 'However, the pressies arrive just the same.' He pulled out a wallet and handed each girl a tenner. 'Is this a warrior game, something like that?' Lane asked, pointing at the poker and tongs.

'She was worried,' Jill said. 'Wanted to ring 999. I ask you. We compromised on this.' She waved the poker. 'Thanks very much, Mr Lane.'

'Some crisis?' Hazel asked. 'Obviously. This venue for a bosky, confidential meeting, you and Dad? Thanks very much, Mr Lane. Hush money?'

'We'll follow you to the house,' Harpur replied. The girls went back.

Lane said: 'Ah, children, so delightful at this season, so indispensable. The Tambo news came early today. Colin, this whole London thing thing disturbs me. Mightily.' He squinted hard at Harpur against the sunlight.

'You're asking, sir, did I see him off, out of posthumous jealousy, and whatever else, in where was it, Careen Street?' Harpur replied.

Lane shrugged, stroked some rhododendron leaves and said: 'Do I understand what is happening?' He shook the fedora. 'There's more, Colin.' He had a sigh and then a mighty shrug. It was all beyond him. 'They looked for other directors, and especially one, a name well known to them, apparently – Clive Thomas Brince, crooked dandy, mid-twenties with addresses in Southall and Peckham. The Peckham garden flat is actually his widowed mother's but he uses it sometimes when she's wintering in Spain. The Met could get no reply at either address but at the Peckham one neighbours said there had been odd happenings yesterday, so they forced entry.'

'They don't mess about, the Met.'

'They don't and others don't. This lad Brince was in there, naked and dead, fixed with padlocked chains to the handle of an underfloor safe and shot three times, twice chest, once head, from no distance. Some mess. Presumably a silenced weapon. It was not heard. My friend at the Yard couldn't hide joy.'

'God, here's a mystery,' Harpur replied. ' "Odd happenings"? What's that mean, sir?'

'They say a man wearing a full-length sable-fur coat and not much else came out.'

'Definitely a man, sir? Not some strippergram stunt? Fancy dress season?'

'Possible wounds or burns on the parts of his legs visible and his bare feet. An ancient Princess was hanging about there all day with varying numbers of unidentified men aboard. Young, tall, scrawny driver. One of the others very big. The charmer in the fur coat left in this car, and the Met got a reg for it from people on the first floor, which is going some for Peckham. The computer says scrapyarded two years ago and has no traceable existence or therefore owner.'

'Shall we go up to the house, sir.'

'You seemed to be hanging a picture, Colin.'

'A gift from a dear aunt who keeps in touch, and loves art. I'll be glad of your view.'

They crossed the lawn, glistening and brittle under the December sun. Harpur was still unsure what he felt about Tambo's death, but, like the Yard man, could not fault the Brince story. It neatly completed a couple of circles, his own and Erogenous's.

Lane said: 'What they're wondering at the Met, naturally, is whether Tambo did this lad at Peckham – trying to break loose from a business hold, or possibly some other grievance – then topped himself. Remorse? And, of course, I don't need to tell you he had other grounds for that, too. Yes. From what I hear, Tambo had noble streaks, though you'd probably question that.'

'Suicide can bring some dignity, sir.'

'Or possibly he disposed of this one but then realized he was still not out of things, as long as Anstical stayed around. Thus, despair? A state I understand, Colin. And he might have thought a body in the flat would give Anstical trouble, which it has and will. Brince was nominally a director of the company but really only Anstical's dogsbody for dirty jobs. Yes: look, the description they give of him, Brince, could easily tie in with Iles's man on the train – the moustache, dark hair and a bit of a dresser, so possibly the fur collar.'

'We must tell the ACC.'

They were at the house and paused outside. Lane leaned against the wall near the french windows which were open and spoke very quietly, so that the girls could not hear. 'It all reaches out to Megan? Does it? I fear so. That might give Tambo another motive, of course – redress for her killing: not all police believe the law can deal adequately with the worst crimes, especially those that touch them personally. Of course, she's not his wife, Colin, yours, but—'

'Yes, I've heard people go it alone, sir.'

'He might have handled this vengeance in his own way and then been unable to live with what he had done. What in God's name is happening, Colin?'

It was the kind of question the Chief sometimes asked, where you did not know whether it was only a baffled cry of grief, or a demand for the information he knew you were sitting on. 'How Tambo if the Magnum's only one round short, sir? And does he have a silencer?'

'A problem, yes. They've no ballistics yet. Perhaps he had another weapon?'

'It's a pit up there.' Harpur watched a robin, fat and jolly-looking enough for a Christmas card, tug at a worm.

'They can account for four leaving in the Princess. If the sable coat was an extra – someone from inside the flat – there should have been five. And possibly even six: one neighbour says a man in a duffle coat and bobble hat hanging about, independent of the Princess party. Tambo's build.'

'Two people left behind then, each of whom might have done this execution? Is that the thinking, sir?'

'It seems. Or jointly. But neither identified, and not much hope, I'm told.'

'Were you asking me if I'd done Tambo, then, sir?'

Lane put a hand gently on Harpur's shoulder, gently so that it would be taken as a clear act of friendship, not an arrest. He said nothing, though.

'No, sir,' Harpur replied.

Lane nodded a couple of times, which could mean, Of course, I accept that, or Jesus, but you would say so. 'And then an inquest. Tambo's messy life gone into. That kind of thing. Good for the police service? The impact on your children?'

'They're pretty hard.'

'I can't believe it.'

'So, do I tell Mr Iles about Tambo, sir, supposing he doesn't know?' The robin had finished the worm and busily looked for more. Well, it was Christmas.

'He can't know. Can he?' Lane replied.

'This is Mr Iles we're talking about, sir.'

'Yes. Well, if he appears not to know don't tell him yet, Colin. I should do that, I think.' They went in through the french windows and Lane stood before the print, acting thorough relish.

'It's Henry Miller, sir. The artist, not the subject. He's better known as a writer, of course, but I've always loved his painting, too – my aunt knowing this.'

Jill gave a bit of a groan and turned it into a cry of delight on pulling the paper from the glossy, lethal Walkman. She switched it on. It had been foolishly tuned in the shop to Radio 4, and a grand old carol greeted them, *Good Christian men, rejoice*. Lane picked up the words in his pleasant, light singing voice. Iles, too, liked doing a carol. Possibly a Coral. Jill had the grace to let the carol and him finish and then swiftly found Radio 1 and rap attack.

'Yes, let's try to rejoice today,' Lane seemed to say, though Harpur had to lip read because of the racket. It almost drowned the telephone bell, too. Harpur put down Megan's shoe, picked up the receiver and waved a silencing hand at Jill. She switched off.

Denise said: 'Happy Christmas, lover. And thanks for the gorgeous gift. How did you know?'

'And a Happy Christmas to you, too.' Window shopping with him in Bond Street she had ignored the big money stuff in a jeweller's window and rhapsodized over a moonstone ring instead, saying there was some book connection. He had not bought it then but detoured in the taxi with Erogenous, on their way back to the station. Harpur loved ways of contacting books without reading.

'You've got people there doing Yule *camaraderie*, Col?'

'Yes.'

'And *Clown*? Like?'

'It's lovely. I've hung it.'

He saw Hazel wearing her new denim top go from the room and probably upstairs to listen on the extension.

'Where?'

'The sitting-room.'

'That where she had the discussions and all that? Her desk? Sort of her special room?'

'Yes.'

'Good. I like it being there then.'

'Where else?'

'Where do you keep her ashes?'

'Oh, not there.'

'Sure?'

'How will you spend the day?' he replied.

'I thought the clown bore a resemblance. Not just the blue nose. Those rather tender *soixante-neuf* lips. I'll try to get down again soon. We must bring in the New Year as it ought to be brought in.'

'So kind.'

Harpur rejoined the Chief in front of the print. Jill hammered the room with Walkman again. 'It's the lips, I like,' Harpur yelled to Lane. 'Vibrant, somehow.' Hazel came back into the room and resumed opening presents. After a couple of minutes, Lane waved to both of the girls through the music and left.

The Ileses did Christmas dinner for 4.30 p.m., and Harpur and his daughters, with Scott and Darren, arrived an hour early, as instructed. They found the ACC had been called away early in the morning but hoped to make it back for the meal. Sarah handed out drinks.

'Called where?' Harpur asked.

'Some situation,' Sarah replied. 'He said he'd circulated nationwide a description of the train man and someone like it has been found dead. Violently dead. He and Francis were going to identify, or not.'

'Where?' Harpur asked.

'He didn't disclose. You're familiar with what he's like. What you're all like. I expect you know where, anyway. You usually know more than he does. It's lovely to see you, Col. Seems an age since—'

'Yes.'

The baby lay in a cot among some scattered newspapers and other clutter on the far side of the room. Hazel and Jill were cooing over her, tickling her, squeaking her toys. The two boys watched Charles Laughton Blighing it in the original *Mutiny on the Bounty* on television. To the side of the set was a portrait in oils of a woman Iles said was an ancestress, which had come down to him through the family. The face definitely had the same kind of bogus sweetness and genuine insolence as the ACC's, and the picture was so dark and dull it seemed impossible anybody would actually buy it, let alone Iles, so possibly he spoke the truth.

'I'm not sure I like to think of you as a widower, Col,' Sarah said. 'Too free.' She was flushed with cookery and drinks and wore old jeans and a loose grey jumper. She looked very young, very much the way she used to.

'I think my daughters consider I was fairly free before.'

'They don't understand these things. Not yet. Soon, though.'

She went out into the kitchen holding her glass of neat gin, to tend the cooking vegetables. He followed, closing the door. The kitchen was at least as unkempt as the living-room. 'Things all right here now, Sarah? I mean, all right?' he asked. He drank white wine, because of the driving. She was blonde, broadening a little, though only a little, and nimble on her feet. She could be very tough, she could be very tender. It had been grand between them not all that long ago.

'Des and me? Yes, things are all right,' she said.

'Good, Sarah.'

'Patronizing sod.'

'I didn't mean it.'

'I could see that.' She stirred a couple of saucepans, then turned. 'Listen, Col, we're a bit pressed, aren't we? I'm going upstairs to change now.'

'I see.'

'I put it off till you got here.'

'Sarah, there's the kids.'

'Mine won't mind. The others are preoccupied. Use the rear stairs.'

'We don't know what time the ACC will be back?'

'The ACC! I told you. For the meal.'

'Yes.' Christ.

'Too bothered about it?'

'Bothered.'

She left the kitchen and, in a moment, he went up the stairs after her. She was already naked in the big bedroom when he arrived, standing next to the frame of a beautiful cheval mirror, which contained no glass.

'I'd like to undress you, Col, but no time.'

'No time at all. Anyway, I've lately learned how to manage buttons.'

In the bed not much longer afterwards she said: 'No, Col, it's not all right here. Not that sort of all right. How could it be? But it will do, you understand. It will do except now and again and especially now. And I expect you have comfort from elsewhere, anyway.' Through the floor from the room below he thought he could hear someone being flogged around the Fleet with drum accompaniment. 'Think I'm getting tubby,' she asked.

'Only in the right regions.'

'Doll.'

She got out of bed and hurriedly dressed, in the same clothes. 'Christ, my swede.'

Harpur dressed, too, and made the bed. He rejoined the children just as Bligh was being cut adrift in the small boat and shouting his fine threat. Sarah told everyone she would delay the meal until 5 p.m., in the hope that Iles would make it. 'Things wouldn't be the same without Des.'

He arrived at 4.50, looking weary, Harpur thought, even dishevelled, yet aglow with Christmas excitement, like one of the Magi, the craftiest one. He was again rich in references to the glorious meaning of the day and shook hands with everyone, including Fanny and Sarah, kissing them both, too. 'Ah, damned intrusive duty, so all the hospitality falls on poor Sarah,' he said. When he reached Harpur, near the oil portrait of the ancestor, he gripped his hand with what seemed to Harpur exceptional seasonal warmth, smiling grandly, and muttered softly: 'You fucking interfering bastard, Harpur. I'll get you yet. You traced him?'

They moved into the dining-room and Sarah emerged from the kitchen with a great silver tureen of turtle soup which she set on the long table. It was covered by three worn-looking tablecloths overlapping one another, and Harpur saw he should have lent them the Irish linen one. The place settings were beautiful. Sarah and Iles did not worry much about furniture or cleanliness or carpets or tablecloths, but Harpur knew both revelled in good crockery, glass and eating irons. Some marriages lacked even that much accord. Jill was at the head of the table, Iles in the middle between Scott and Sarah. Hazel had seemed edgy until Iles arrived, but was happier now, Scott no.

Sarah said: 'Colin brought a couple of 1971 Pomerol. Do with the goose, Des? I've pulled the corks.'

'Great,' Iles replied. 'Go with anything. Col knows his way around. I've always said that. I heard the Queen on the car radio and people can laugh but this was a passable trot of wordage, especially thinking of her family. Those poor Personal Protection coppers. Who'd want proximity to that palace litter?'

Darren said: 'But surely the Royal Family is under exceptional pressure.'

'I've heard that,' Iles replied. 'I'm on their side. Help me cart in some of the vegetables, Col, will you?' In the kitchen, the ACC said: 'Someone got to him, then.'

'Which one is that, sir?'

'You know the site? This is some so-called garden flat. A basement dungeon.'

'A lot of them have plants around and so on. They can give a garden feel.'

'You actually went there, did you, you sod? I thought so. Whose bloody car, this resurrected wreck? Who else? They've got nothing, nothing except a corpse, and won't get anything.'

'This was what you were called to, sir? And on Christmas morn. It's harsh.'

'I look at this creepy object chained and destroyed and I have to wonder: you? Tambo? Erogenous? Well, you're here, to be asked. The other two we have to find, haven't we? Tambo's not at Highbury-cum-Islington, so where the hell? Or, then again, there's this huge character in the passenger seat of the Princess. Grosser than you, I mean. It's not my problem, though. Not my patch.'

'Erogenous is home, I think, sir. Back from the warehouse inquiries and resting up. He's so grateful about the promotion.'

'Get hold of this,' Iles replied, passing a serving dish of mushrooms. 'And who the hell told you about Pomerol 1971, Harpur?'

They made a combined ceremonial entry with the food, Iles pushing a tottering old wooden serving trolley, the goose on its upper level, looking huge and magnificently golden. Harpur carried a laden tray. Iles took his suit jacket off, made a hole in the middle of the front and back pages of an old *Telegraph* through which he pushed his head, creating an apron, and began to carve and distribute. 'I always think of that bitchy scene at the start of *Portrait of the Artist* when doing this, don't you, Harpur?'

'Just get on with it, will you?' Sarah replied. 'No tour of your hackneyed mind.'

'You've an appetite, have you, love?' Iles said.

'It's a real feast,' Harpur replied.

When the port was on the table, Iles, still wearing newspaper, stood and quietly made a toast: 'To the memory of Megan Harpur,' he said. 'A pure woman.'

'Right on,' Sarah replied. 'Pure woman.'

'The whole matter has been more or less closed for me today,' Iles said. 'Finished.'

'Oh?' Sarah replied.

'But don't ask me about it. Ask Colin, who'll tell you nothing.'

'To the memory of Megan Harpur,' Scott said, and they stood and drank.

Hazel said: 'Thanks, Des Iles.'

Darren said: 'I'm so glad I came. What I feel here

above all, today, Christmas, is a lovely sense of, well, like family.'

'As at that wondrous first Christmas,' Iles replied.

'So, do you know now exactly what happened to my mother, Mr Iles?' Jill asked.

Chapter 44

Bent over the lock in the car park, Megan heard the footsteps, undisguised and swift, behind and did not look around but hurried to get the door open. Crazily, a line from *Endgame* on that earlier trip rushed her mind: *This is what we called making an exit.* A hand grabbed her shoulder and pulled her up straight and around so she saw the fur collar, the moustache, the knife.

'Christ,' she screamed. 'I thought you fancied me.'

'But there's work to do,' he replied.